College English

Fast

Reading

Coursebook

大学英语
快速阅读教程

总主编：秦 旭　总主审：俞洪亮

本册主编：朱建新
本册副主编：李葆春　田 杰

4

外语教学与研究出版社
FOREIGN LANGUAGE TEACHING AND RESEARCH PRESS
北京 BEIJING

图书在版编目(CIP)数据

大学英语快速阅读教程 = College English Fast Reading Coursebook. 4 / 秦旭主编；朱建新分册主编 .— 北京：外语教学与研究出版社，2009.10
ISBN 978 - 7 - 5600 - 9095 - 5

Ⅰ. 大⋯　Ⅱ. ①秦⋯ ②朱⋯　Ⅲ. 英语—阅读教学—高等学校—教材　Ⅳ. H319.4

中国版本图书馆 CIP 数据核字 (2009) 第 187000 号

universal tool·unique value·useful source·unanimous choice

 悠游外语网
www.2u4u.com.cn

外研社全新推出读者增值服务网站，独家打造双语互动资源

欢迎你：
○ 随时检测个人的外语水平和专项能力
○ 在线阅读外语读物、学习外语网络课程
○ 在线观看双语视频、名家课堂、外语系列讲座
○ 下载外语经典图书、有声读物、学习软件、翻译软件
○ 参与社区互动小组，参加线上各种比赛和联谊活动
○ 咨询在线专家，解决外语学习中的疑难问题

此外，你还可以通过积累购书积分，兑换图书、电子书、培训课程和其他增值服务⋯⋯

你有你"优"，你的优势就是你的拥有。即刻登录，抢先体验！

出 版 人：于春迟
责任编辑：连　静
美术编辑：蔡　颖
出版发行：外语教学与研究出版社
社　　址：北京市西三环北路 19 号 (100089)
网　　址：http://www.fltrp.com
印　　刷：北京爱丽龙印刷有限责任公司
开　　本：787×1092　1/16
印　　张：6.5
版　　次：2009 年 10 月第 1 版　2009 年 10 月第 1 次印刷
书　　号：ISBN 978 - 7 - 5600 - 9095 - 5
定　　价：13.00 元
＊　　＊　　＊

前　言

　　有效地提高学生的阅读速度以及培养学生的阅读能力一直是大学英语教学中的一个非常重要的环节。2004年，教育部启动了全国大学英语教学改革工作，明确提出了培养学生英语综合应用能力的教学目标。《大学英语快速阅读教程》即是根据大学英语教学改革的精神并依照教育部2007年9月颁布的《大学英语课程教学要求》中关于阅读能力培养的"一般要求"和"较高要求"的目标而编写的一套快速阅读教材。

　　英语综合应用能力是一个整体概念，是听、说、读、写等几种能力的有机结合。大学英语在教学定位时强调突出听说能力的训练，但绝不是要忽视或者削弱读写能力的培养。英语阅读能力是在大量阅读实践中培养的，对阅读的要求，首先是理解，其次是速度。培养英语阅读能力三个至关重要的因素包括阅读材料的选取、阅读策略的培养以及阅读速度的提高。在扩大阅读范围、提高阅读技能的同时，要充分挖掘快速阅读的潜力，这样的阅读活动，不但可以激发阅读的兴趣和动机，满足英语学习的成就感，而且还可以培养发现问题、解决问题的能力，也可以提高英语交际能力和自主学习的能力。

　　《大学英语快速阅读教程》充分研究了国内外英语快速阅读教材的编写原则和特点，吸纳了同类教材的长处和优点。教材在选材理念、内容体系、练习设计等方面主要体现如下几个特点：

　　一是在材料的选择上，既注意题材的人文性和科学性，又考虑选材的趣味性和实用性；既重视语言的可读性，又强调选材对学生跨文化交际意识的积累和培养。阅读材料的体裁主要是议论文、记叙文、说明文、科普作品等。每个单元涉及同一个话题，包括外语学习、校园生活、社会生活、娱乐时尚、文化、历史、教育、经济、传媒、计算机网络、外国地理、西方风情、体育、自然、灾害、环保、科技、旅游、艺术、留学、名人等内容，体现了"语言是文化的载体"这一重要理念。

　　二是在内容体系的安排上，与新的《大学英语课程教学要求》中关于阅读能力的"一般要求"和"较高要求"的目标全面接轨，满足分层次教学的需要。全套教材共128篇文章，其中每册8单元，每单元4篇；每单元含Section A和Section B两部分，每部分含Passage 1和Passage 2。全部文章均采用以词频为基础设计的词汇统计软件程序——RANGE进行了自动评估，分析比较了不同文本的词汇量大小、措辞的异同和词汇的复现率等，然后按照语篇的长度和难度进行了分类和分级。1至4册语言难度逐步提高，其中每册各单元Section B中的两篇文章的长度和难度均大于Section A中的两篇文章。各册每单元1至4篇文章的长度分别控制在350-450词、450-550词、550-650词和650-800词左右。对部分词汇作了简化处理，即用更常见的单词替换了原来难度较大的单词；对影响阅读理解的超出课程要求的词汇或短语在首次出现时在文中进行了汉语注释；对不影响阅读理解的超出课程要求的词汇不作注释，鼓励学生根据上下文对词义进行猜测。对文章中出现的个别专有名词、词组或者缩略语在文后进行了注释。每个单元有一段英文导读，阐释本单元的主题，引导学生对阅读材料进行整体思考和把握。

三是在练习的设计上，既注重打好语言基础，又强化阅读理解能力的综合训练，特别是多样化的题型充分体现了快速阅读的策略和特点。练习的设计围绕略读（skimming）、寻读（scanning）和判断等策略，训练学生进行猜词悟义、文章主旨判断、特定信息寻找、行文顺序安排、文章大意概括、小标题或者主题句与内容对应、事实或者观点辨析等快速阅读能力的培养。

每篇文章后标出了具体的单词数，目的是让学生按照《大学英语课程教学要求》中关于阅读能力培养的"一般要求"和"较高要求"的目标进行训练。阅读理解能力的"一般要求"是："能基本读懂一般性题材的英文文章，阅读速度达到每分钟70词。在快速阅读篇幅较长、难度略低的材料时，阅读速度达到每分钟100词。能就阅读材料进行略读和寻读。能借助词典阅读本专业的英语教材和题材熟悉的英文报刊文章，掌握中心大意，理解主要事实和有关细节。能读懂工作、生活中常见的应用文体的材料。能在阅读中使用有效的阅读方法。"阅读理解能力的"较高要求"是："能基本读懂英语国家大众性报刊杂志上一般性题材的文章，阅读速度为每分钟70-90词。在快速阅读篇幅较长、难度适中的材料时，阅读速度达到每分钟120词。能阅读所学专业的综述性文献，并能正确理解中心大意，抓住主要事实和有关细节。"因此，在使用本教材时，可以将100词/分钟设定为"一般要求"的目标阅读时间，将120词/分钟设定为"较高要求"的目标阅读时间。按照每篇的单词数和自己的实际阅读时间计算出自己的阅读速度，并且将自己的实际阅读时间和目标阅读时间进行对照，寻找差距，循序渐进，逐步提高阅读速度。

本套教材是集体智慧的结晶。全套教材的文章选题、内容安排以及练习题型设计由秦旭总策划并担任总主编，秦旭、王骏编写了各个单元的英文导读，王毅负责文本词汇的评估和分级。全套教材由秦旭、王骏负责初审，俞洪亮担任总审。秦旭、王维倩、邓笛、朱建新分别担任第一、二、三、四册主编。

本套教材是江苏省高等教育教改立项研究重点课题"地方综合性高校学生英语综合应用能力培养模式与途径"（苏教高[2007] 18号）的成果之一。外语教学与研究出版社的编辑们在整套教材的编写、策划、版式设计等方面做了大量工作，在此，编者表示感谢。

本套教材是我们在大学英语教学内容和课程体系改革方面所作的一次努力，其中定会存在不当和疏漏之处，敬请使用者批评指正。

编者
2009年6月

Contents

Unit One

Lead-in

Have you ever kept a pet like a dog, a cat or even some exotic (奇异的) animals? Feeling the ever mounting pressure from the crazy pace of life, the modern people are inclined to keep one pet or another. They take it as a source of comfort, love, loyalty or simply companionship. While offering something of human warmth, however, a pet may also cause the problems like disease or danger. One problem in particular is the overwhelming sense of loss felt by many people after their pets were lost or died. To help them get over the deep sorrow is of as much a social issue as helping those suffering the loss of their child. The attachment to pets, as a matter of fact, is the symptom of the deep loneliness felt by many modern people.

 **Section A**

Passage One

My Pet Rabbit

My rabbit's name is Bugs and he was given to me by my friend Nancy. Bugs was left out in the woods by his previous owner and Nancy found him. Knowing I had a six-year-old daughter, Nancy asked if I would like the rabbit for her. I picked the rabbit up from her house and brought him home. My daughter was delighted, but all I kept thinking was "What am I going to do with this thing now that we have him?".

The first week was the hardest. My rabbit was 4-6 months old when we got him and was left abandoned in the woods. Bugs was very skittish (易受惊的) and needed to get used to us and his new environment. During the second week, he was much better. He started taking food from our hands, would let us pick him up and hold him without trying to get away and would hop over to us when he was out of his cage. A little love, trust and patience will go a long way. Here are three things you should do if you want your rabbit to befriend you.

1. Make sure you have a proper cage for your rabbit.

I recommend having a cage that has both a top and side door. Having two doors is important. The top door is useful when you first get your rabbit because you can slowly reach in and pet him without scaring him or worrying that he might get out. Eventually, you will have your rabbit trained to go into and out of the cage on his own. His cage should be big enough for him to have a "living" area and a "potty" area. Tall cages with a ramp (人造斜坡) leading up to a stoop (门廊) are very good since it gives them an area to sit and they get exercise going up and down the ramp. Don't forget to have hay or a mat or both for them to rest on.

2. Let your rabbit exercise every day.

I suggest having a small confined space to allow the rabbit to hop around. It was May when we got Bugs so I would take him out on the front porch and let him hop around. The kitchen is the best indoor area. Usually there is nothing down low (like electrical cords [电线]) for them to get hurt with and you have a clear and clean floor when they go to the bathroom. Use a baby gate to block the doorway. You should have your rabbit out to exercise 1-2 times a day for 30-60 minutes. An exercise pen ([饲养家畜的]圈，栏) is an excellent way to keep your rabbit safe indoors and out.

3. Feed your rabbit well.

You should feed your rabbit a combination of fruits, vegetables and dry food three times a day. Also try to have the rabbit take a piece of food from your hand each time you feed him. This will help build trust between you and your rabbit. Experiment with different rabbit treats in between feedings. You will find that your rabbit has one or two favorite treats. My rabbit loves blueberry yogurt treats.

(550 words)

Exercises

For questions1-6, complete the sentences with the information given in the passage.

1. When the author got his rabbit, it was _____ and _____.

2. In the first week at the author's home, the rabbit was _____ and _____.

3. _____ will go a long way in getting along with the rabbit.

4. Tall cages with a ramp leading up to a stoop are very good since it gives the rabbit _____.

5. _____ is the best indoor area for the author's rabbit to hop round.

6. To help build trust between the owner and the rabbit, the owner had better _____ each time the owner feeds the rabbit.

▶ ***For questions 7-10, read the following statements, mark Y (for YES) if the statement agrees with the information given in the passage; N (for NO) if the statement contradicts the information given in the passage; NG (for NOT GIVEN) if the information is not given in the passage.***

_____ 7. It's easy to raise the rabbit in the beginning because he was tame.

_____ 8. Either side of the cage of the author's rabbit has a small door on it.

_____ 9. The author confines his rabbit to a small indoor area for him to exercise, since it will run away outdoors.

_____ 10. The author put the food on a small tray before the rabbit to feed him.

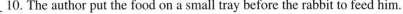 *Passage Two*

The Most Dangerous Pets

Most countries have laws against them. In most places around the globe, it is illegal to capture, breed, or sell them. Yet worldwide there is a fascination with owning wild, bizarre (古怪的), exotic, and most of the time dangerous pets. What are this fascination with being different and the need to own something illegal and dangerous? Who owns these animals? And, what are these animals that are owned, sold, and traded worldwide regardless of the consequences?

Born Free U.S.A. united with Animal Protection Institute issued a report of incidents involving captive held animals, which provided an interesting background report to base the list upon. There are also stories like this in papers around the world concerning the practice of keeping dangerous and exotic pets.

10. Turtles

A turtle may seem harmless enough, but do you know that they actually carry salmonella (沙门氏菌)? It seems that the main concern is the baby turtles. It is not that the little guys have more cases of salmonella; it's that the smaller they are the more attracted little kids are to them. And we all know how little kids can be; they will stick just about anything in their mouth—including their fingers after touching the turtles and the turtles themselves.

9. Constrictors (蟒蛇)

This is pretty much an obvious one. Sure that red tailed boa (蟒蛇) at the pet store seems harmless and kind of cute. But they grow quite rapidly; can get up to several feet in length, and speaking from a neighborhood experience, they have been known to escape. Let's just say if you feed them rabbits, they would have no problem with getting themselves around a dog or a cat even. One of the main concerns with owning constrictors is that once they start to get large, some people actually just let them go and return them to the wild. Watch out for Fido!

8. Scorpions (蝎子)

Did you know that there is a guy who, as a performer and a world record chaser, actually puts live Scorpions in his mouth? If you ask me, that's not one of the best ideas I have heard of. Seeing the little ones when I lived in the southern U.S. was enough for me. These little guys can pack quite a punch with their venomous sting!

7. Camels

Camels are known to be temperamental guys. According to a report on "Fox News" when a local TV news crew was out filming exotic animal farms, an 1,800-pound camel named Polo must have decided that they were not shooting his best side. When Polo became agitated he attacked his owner, kicking her and sitting on her. Ouch. Oh, and if you didn't know, camels like to spit too. And it's pretty gross.

6. Ostriches (鸵鸟)

Sure they seem stupid and are awkward-looking. They hide their heads in the ground right. But apparently these guys will also chase you and they run pretty darn (特别地) fast. Getting in the middle of an ostrich stampede ([受惊动物的]奔逃，逃窜) just doesn't sound like my idea of a really good time.

5. Chimps and Monkeys

They are adorable. The human resemblance is amazing. They are also known to bite and attack. I once saw the damage that a monkey caused when it attacked a dog in India and let's just say those puncture wounds weren't pretty. The dog also lost an ear and an eye in the process. Sometimes cuteness is pretty deceptive.

4. Venomous Snakes

Again I go back to my comments about the scorpions. They are snakes. They are poisonous. They bite. None of this is a good combination. In Cincinnati, a man was bitten by his rhinoceros viper (犀角蝰), which is one of the world's deadliest snakes. He did receive anti-venom (抗毒血清) and survived. But who really wants to take that risk?

3. Crocodiles and Alligators (短鼻鳄鱼)

Often people get crocs and alligators when they are little and cute and look like happy little lizards (蜥蜴). Have you seen the jaws (颚) on those things? They didn't make an entire TV show around hunting them out if there wasn't some sort of risk and danger there. So keeping one in a kiddy pool in the back yard may not be the best idea. Just ask anyone who has lived in Florida and found one under their car.

2. Big Cats ([狮子、虎等]大型猫科运动)

Again it's these cute ones that you have to worry about. When these guys are babies, who could resist? But no matter how young they are or how well trained they are, they can turn on you in a second. They feed them raw steak for goodness sake; shouldn't that be a sign?

1. Kinkajous (蜜熊)

OK, so I had no idea what a kinkajou even was. But when I looked it up I couldn't resist its adorable little furry bodies and those big buggy eyes. A kinkajou, also known as a sugar bear, looks like a cross between a squirrel, a hamster (仓鼠), and a chinchilla (栗鼠). They are pretty darn cute. But again it's the cute ones. Paris Hilton has a pet kinkajou named Baby Luv. In 2005 she took it shopping with her and was attacked by the thing and it clawed up her face. The brilliance of this is that again in 2006 Baby Luv sent Hilton to the emergency room after she was bitten by that cute Baby Luv on the arm. And that is why this guy is number one on my list of dangerous pets.

(987 words)

Exercises

For questions 1-8, choose the best answer from the four choices marked A), B), C) and D) according to the information given in the passage.

1. Salmonella is most probably _____.
   A) a tucked-in claw   B) a feeler
   C) a kind of bacteria   D) a fang

2. Among the unfortunate incidents related by the author, which animal's victim is not a human?
   A) The venomous Snakes.   B) The camel.
   C) The kinkajou.   D) The monkey.

3. According to the author, the camel was temperamental, because _____.
   A) it was not fed well
   B) people didn't bring its beauty to the full when filming it
   C) it was exhausted
   D) it was beaten

4. Which of these animals would stampede?
   A) Big cats.   B) Ostriches.
   C) Camels.   D) Crocodiles and alligators.

5. Which of these animals are little but poisonous?
   A) Kinkajous.   B) Chimps and monkeys.
   C) Constrictors.   D) Scorpions.

6. Many animals in the list are dangerous but cute, and which animals are not one of them?
   A) Ostriches.   B) Chimps and monkeys.
   C) Big cats.   D) Kinkajous.

7. Which of these animals have a resemblance to humans?
   A) Kinkajous.   B) Chimps and monkeys.
   C) Turtles.   D) Big cats.

8. Which of these animals have a resemblance to three other species at the same time?
   A) Chimps and monkeys.   B) Scorpions.
   C) Constrictors.   D) Kinkajous.

▶ *For questions 9-10, there are three definitions below each underlined word in the passage. One definition is closest to its meaning. One definition has the opposite or nearly opposite meaning. The remaining definition has a completely different meaning. Label the definitions C for closest, O for opposite, and D for different.*

9. These little guys can pack quite a punch with their <u>venomous</u> sting!
   _____ A) poisonous
   _____ B) obnoxious
   _____ C) innocuous

10. When Polo became <u>agitated</u> he attacked his owner, kicking her and sitting on her.
    _____ A) calm

_____ B) nervous
_____ C) defeated

Section B

Passage One

Making Peace Between Dogs and Cats

Most dogs can be taught to tolerate cats if their owners are willing to be patient and consistent. Some dogs take longer to train than others and the difference is usually due to the dog's level of "prey drive (猎物驱动)".

Nature designed canines (犬) to be predators (食肉动物)—to chase and catch smaller animals for food. Although dogs have been domesticated for thousands of years, they still act upon the instincts nature gave them. Through generations of selective breeding, people have modified these instincts. By decreasing the effects of some and enhancing the effects of others, we've been able to develop a wide variety of different breeds of dogs, each meant to serve a different purpose or perform a certain function.

A dog's instinct to chase and catch something is called his "prey drive". Throw a stuffed toy for a puppy and watch his prey drive in action as he chases it, catches it, and then shakes it to "kill" it. Breeds and individual dogs vary in the intensity of their prey drives. Breeds created specifically for killing other animals—most terriers (小猎犬), for example, were intended to kill rats—have very high prey drives.

In other breeds, the prey drive has been altered to suit an entirely different purpose. In the Border Collie (边境牧羊犬), a herding breed, the instinct to chase and catch animals has been modified to chase and gather them together. Prey drive can also be modified by training. Drug-sniffing and arson-detection dogs (缉毒犬和搜爆犬) have high prey drives that have been redirected toward objects—these dogs are taught that illegal drugs and fire accelerants are "prey". Although we think of the Greyhound (灵缇) as a racing dog, it was originally bred for hunting, using its great speed to chase down hares (野兔) and other fast creatures. Consequently, it has a high prey drive and is inclined to chase cats.

There are several effective ways to train a dog with a high prey drive to live peacefully with cats or other small pets. I prefer to teach these dogs that cats are off limits altogether and are not to be disturbed. Using a friend or family member to help you, set up several short daily training sessions. With the dog wearing a training collar and leash ([牵狗的]绳子), put him on a sit/stay beside you. Have your friend hold the cat on the other side of the room. Your dog will probably be very curious and even excited at seeing the cat, but insist that he remain in the sit/stay position. Praise your dog for sitting calmly.

Have your friend bring the cat a few steps closer. If your dog continues to stay quietly at your side, wonderful! Praise him for it. If he tries to lunge at the cat, though, give him a stern, fierce-sounding "NO! LEAVE IT!" along with a short, sharp jerk on the leash and put him back in the sit/stay position. As soon as he is sitting calmly again, praise him sincerely. Continue bringing the cat closer, a few feet at a time, repeating the corrections as needed and making sure to praise the dog when he sits quietly and ignores the cat. Have patience—depending on the intensity of your dog, you might only be able to gain a few feet each session.

When your dog is able to sit calmly even when the cat is right next to him, you're ready to proceed to the next step. Release the dog from his sit/stay and let him walk around the room with the cat present. Leave his leash on so you can easily catch him and give the necessary correction if he gives any sign of wanting to chase the cat. Your supervision at this point is critical—to be effective, you must be able to correct the dog each and every time he even thinks about going after the cat. If he's allowed to chase her, even once, he'll want to try it again and you'll have to start your training over from the beginning.

Some dogs learn quickly, others may take weeks to become trustworthy around cats. Until you're sure the dog will remember his training, don't leave them together unsupervised!

(733 words)

Exercises

For questions 1-6, read the following statements, mark Y (for YES) if the statement agrees with the information given in the passage; N (for NO) if the statement contradicts the information given in the passage; NG (for NOT GIVEN) if the information is not given in the passage.

_____ 1. People have been able to develop a wide variety of different breeds of dogs by modifying their instincts.

_____ 2. All the breeds of dogs have a strong level of prey drive, and that's the reason why cats are chased by them.

_____ 3. Only in the sit/stay position can a dog be kept from chasing a cat.

_____ 4. Dogs can be taught to leave cats alone because their instincts have undergone fundamental changes.

_____ 5. All the dogs can be taught to coexist with cats peacefully.

_____ 6. You need to be watchful when your dog is around cats unless you are sure that your dog has learnt to leave cats alone.

▶ *For questions 7-10, there are three definitions below each underlined word in the passage. One definition is closest to its meaning. One definition has the opposite or nearly opposite meaning. The remaining definition has a completely different meaning. Label the definitions C for closest, O for opposite, and D for different.*

7. Although dogs have been <u>domesticated</u> for thousands of years, they still act upon the instincts nature gave them.

     _____ A) untamed

     _____ B) tamed

     _____ C) wiped out

8. Drug-sniffing and arson-detection dogs have high prey drives that have been redirected toward objects—these dogs are taught that illegal drugs and fire <u>accelerants</u> are "prey".

     _____ A) activator

     _____ B) attendee

     _____ C) retardation

9. If he tries to <u>lunge</u> at the cat, though, give him a stern, fierce-sounding "NO! LEAVE IT!" along with a short, sharp jerk on the leash and put him back in the sit/stay position.

     _____ A) recoil

     _____ B) faint

     _____ C) attack

10. Your <u>supervision</u> at this point is critical—to be effective, you must be able to correct the dog cach and every time he even thinks about going after the cat.

     _____ A) indulgence

     _____ B) superiority

     _____ C) direction

Passage Two

How to Deal with the Loss of Your Pet

When a person you love dies, it's natural to feel sorrow, express grief, and expect friends and family to provide understanding and comfort.

Unfortunately, the same doesn't always hold true if the one who died was your companion animal. Many consider grieving inappropriate for someone who has lost "just a pet". Nothing could be further from the truth.

Members of the Family

People love their pets and consider them members of their family. Caregivers celebrate their pets' birthdays, confide in their animals, and carry pictures of them in their wallets.

So when your beloved pet dies, it's not unusual to feel overwhelmed by the intensity of your sorrow.

Animals provide companionship, acceptance, emotional support, and unconditional love during the time they share with you. If you understand and accept this bond between humans and animals, you've already taken the first step toward coping with pet loss: knowing that it is okay to grieve when your pet dies.

Understanding how you grieve and finding ways to cope with your loss can bring you closer to the day when memories bring smiles instead of tears.

What Is the Grief Process?

The grief process is as individual as the person, lasting days for one person or years for another. The process typically begins with denial, which offers protection until individuals can realize their loss. Some caregivers may try bargaining with a higher power, themselves, or even their pet to restore life. Some feel anger, which may be directed at anyone involved with the pet, including family, friends, and veterinarians (兽医). Caregivers may also feel guilt about what they did or did not do, and may feel that it is inappropriate to be so upset.

After these feelings subside, caregivers may experience true sadness or grief. They may become withdrawn or depressed.

Acceptance occurs when they accept the reality of their loss and remember their animal companion with decreasing sadness.

Remember, not everyone follows these classic stages of grief—some may skip or repeat a stage, or experience the stages in a different order.

What Can I Do for My Child?

The loss of a pet may be a child's first experience with death. The child may blame himself, his parents, or the veterinarian for not saving the pet.

And he may feel guilty, depressed, and frightened that others he loves may be taken from him.

Trying to protect your child by saying the pet ran away could cause your child to expect the pet's return and feel betrayed after discovering the truth. Expressing your own grief may reassure your child that sadness is okay and help him work through his feelings.

Is the Process More Difficult if I'm a Senior?

Coping with the loss of a pet can be particularly hard for seniors. Those who live alone may feel a loss of purpose and an immense emptiness. The pet's death may also trigger painful memories of other losses and remind caregivers of their own mortality. What's more, the decision to get another pet is complicated by the possibility that the pet may outlive (比……活得长) the caregiver, and hinges on (取决于) the person's physical and financial ability to care for a new pet.

For all these reasons, it's critical that senior pet owners take immediate steps to cope with their loss and regain a sense of purpose. If you are a senior, try interacting with friends and family, calling a pet loss support hotline, even volunteering at a local humane society (保护动物协会).

(598 words)

Exercises

For questions 1-6, complete the sentences with the information given in the passage.

1. Pets can provide their owners with _____.
2. The grief process is generally divided into _____ (how many) stages.
3. Not everyone follows these classic stages of grief—some may _____.

4. When a pet dies, parents should not try to protect their child by saying the pet ran away, because _____.

5. When a pet dies, seniors who live alone may feel _____.

6. For seniors to cope with their loss of pets, they should _____.

▶ *For questions 7-10, there are three definitions below each underlined word in the passage. One definition is closest to its meaning. One definition has the opposite or nearly opposite meaning. The remaining definition has a completely different meaning. Label the definitions C for closest, O for opposite, and D for different.*

7. Many consider grieving <u>inappropriate</u> for someone who has lost "just a pet". Nothing could be further from the truth.

_____ A) improbable

_____ B) suitable

_____ C) unfitting

8. If you understand and accept this bond between humans and animals, you've already taken the first step toward coping with pet loss: knowing that it is okay to <u>grieve</u> when your pet dies.

_____ A) greed

_____ B) celebrate

_____ C) mourn

9. After these feelings <u>subside</u>, caregivers may experience true sadness or grief.

_____ A) intensify

_____ B) fade away

_____ C) subjugate

10. For all these reasons, it's critical that senior pet owners take immediate steps to cope with their loss and <u>regain</u> a sense of purpose.

_____ A) recover

_____ B) bemoan

_____ C) lose

Unit Two

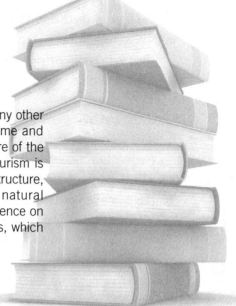

Lead-in

Tourism is now a booming industry in China as well as in many other countries. Tourists, as is widely welcome, promise huge income and play a positive role in preserving and promoting the local culture of the places they visit. Along with the benefits it brings, however, tourism is also plagued by more and more problems such as poor infrastructure, dreadful service, child labor or the increasing strain on natural resources. An equal but less visible problem is the overdependence on tourist industry as a source of financial revenue in many places, which is no doubt an unsustainable mode of development.

 **Section A**

Passage One

The Great Wall

The Great Wall, like the Pyramids of Egypt, the Taj Mahal (泰姬陵) in India and the Hanging Garden of Babylon (巴比伦的空中花园), is one of the great wonders of the world.

Starting out in the east on the banks of the Yalu River in Liaoning Province, the Wall stretches westwards for 12,700 kilometers to Jiayuguan in the Gobi (戈壁) desert, thus known as the Ten Thousand Li Wall in China. The Wall climbs up and down, twists and turns along the ridges of the Yanshan and Yinshan Mountain Chains through five provinces—Liaoning, Hebei, Beijing, Tianjin, Shanxi, Shaanxi, and Gansu—and two autonomous regions—Ningxia and Inner Mongolia, binding the northern China together.

Historical records trace the construction of the Wall to defensive fortification (要塞) back to the year 656 B.C. Its construction continued throughout the Warring States period in the fifth century B.C. when ducal states (诸侯国)Yan, Zhao, Wei, and Qin were frequently plundered by the nomadic (游牧的) people living north of the Yinshan and Yanshan mountain ranges. Walls, then, were built separately by these ducal states to ward off (阻挡) such harassments (骚扰). Later in 221 B.C., when Qin conquered the other states and unified China, Emperor Qinshihuang ordered the connection of these individual walls and further extensions. As a matter of fact, a separate outer wall was constructed north of the Yinshan range in the Han Dynasty (206 B.C.-220 A.D.), which went to ruin through years of neglect. In the many intervening centuries, succeeding dynasties rebuilt parts of the Wall. The most extensive reinforcements and renovations were carried out in the Ming Dynasty (1368-1644) when altogether 18 lengthy stretches were reinforced with bricks and rocks. It is mostly the Ming Dynasty Wall that visitors see today.

The Great Wall is divided into two sections, the east and the west. The west part is a rammed (冲压的) earth construction, about 5.3 meters high on average. In the eastern part, the core of the Wall is rammed earth as well, but the outer shell is reinforced with bricks and rocks. The most imposing and best preserved sections of the Great Wall are at Badaling and Mutianyu, not far from Beijing and both are open to visitors.

The Wall of those sections is 7.8 meters high and 6.5 meters wide at its base, narrowing to 5.8 meters on the ramparts (防御土墙), wide enough for five horses to gallop (奔跑) abreast (并排). There are ramparts, embrasures (炮眼), peep-holes (窥视孔) and apertures (孔) for archers (弓箭手) on the top, besides gutters with gargoyles (滴水嘴) to drain rain-water off the parapet walk. Two-storied watch-towers are built at approximately 400-meter internals. The top stories of the watch-tower were designed for observing enemy movements, while the first was used for storing grain, fodder (饲料), military equipment and gunpowder as well as for quartering garrison (守备) soldiers. The highest watch-tower at Badaling standing on a hill-top, is reached only after a steep climb, like "climbing a ladder to heaven". The view from the top is rewarding, however. The Wall follows the contour (轮廓) of mountains that rise one behind the other until they finally fade and merge with distant haze (烟雾).

A signal system formerly existed that served to communicate military information to the dynastic capital. This consisted of beacon (烽火) towers on the Wall itself and on mountain tops within sight of the Wall. At the approach of enemy troops, smoke signals gave the alarm from the beacon towers in the daytime and bonfire (篝火) did this at night. Emergency signals could be relayed to the capital from distant places within a few hours long before the invention of anything like modern communications.

There stand 14 major passes (Guan, in Chinese) at places of strategic importance along the Great Wall, the most important being Shanhaiguan and Jiayuguan. Yet the most impressive one is Juyongguan, about 50 kilometers northwest of Beijing.

Known as "Tianxia Diyi Guan" (The First Pass Under Heaven), Shanhaiguan Pass is situated between two sheer cliffs forming a neck connecting north China with the northeast. It had been, therefore, a key junction contested by all strategists and many famous battles were fought here. It was the gate of Shanhaiguan that the Ming general Wu Sangui opened to the Manchu army to suppress the peasant rebellion led by Li Zicheng and so surrendered the whole Ming empire to the Manchus, leading to the foundation of the Qing Dynasty (1644-1911).

Jiayuguan Pass was not so much as the "Strategic Pass Under the Heaven" as an important communication center in Chinese history. Cleft (裂口) between the snow-capped Qilian Mountains and the rolling Mazong Mountains, it was on the ancient Silk Road. Zhang Qian, the first envoy of Emperor Wu Di of the Western Han Dynasty (206 B.C.-25 A.D.), crossed it on his journey to the western regions. Later, silk flowed to the west through this pass too. The gate-tower of Jiayuguan is an attractive building of excellent workmanship. It has an inner city and an outer city, the former square in shape and surrounded by a wall 11.7 meters high and 730 meters in circumference. It has two gates, an eastern one and a western one. On each gate sits a tower facing each other. The four corners of the wall are occupied by four watch towers, one for each.

Juyongguan, a gateway to ancient Beijing from Inner Mongolia, was built in a 15-kilometer-long ravine flanked by mountains. The cavalrymen of Genghis Khan swept through it in the 13th century. At the center of the pass is a white marble platform named the Cloud Terrace, which was called the Crossing-Street Dagoba (舍利塔) since its narrow arch spanned the main street of the pass and on the top of the terrace there used to be three stone dagobas, built in the Yuan Dynasty (1206-1368). At the bottom of the terrace is a half-octagonal arch gateway, interesting for its wealth of details: it is decorated with splendid images of Buddha and four celestial guardians carved on the walls. The vividness of their expressions is matched by the exquisite workmanship. Such grandiose relics works, with several stones pieced together, are rarely seen in ancient Chinese carving. The gate jambs bear a multi-lingual Buddhist sutra, carved some 600 years ago in Sanskrit (梵语), Tibetan, Mongolian, Uigur (维吾尔语), Han Chinese and the language of Western Xia. Undoubtedly, they are valuable to the study of Buddhism and ancient languages.

As a cultural heritage, the Wall belongs not only to China but to the world. The Venice charter says: "Historical and cultural architecture not only includes the individual architectural works, but also the urban or rural environment that witnessed certain civilizations, significant social developments or historical events." The Great Wall is the largest of such historical and cultural architecture, and that is why it continues to be so attractive to people all over the world. In 1987, the Wall was listed by UNESCO① as a world cultural heritage site. (1253 words)

Note:

① UNESCO 是 United Nations Educational, Scientific and Cultural Organization （联合国教育、科学及文化组织，简称联合国教科文组织）的简称。

Exercises

For questions 1-6, choose the best answer from the four choices marked A), B), C) and D) according to the information given in the passage.

1. The Great Wall is one of the great _____ of the world.
   A) words   B) wonders   C) walls   D) victories
2. It is _____ that conquered the other ducal states and connected the walls.
   A) Ming   B) Qin   C) Yan   D) Wei
3. As a matter of fact, a separate outer wall was constructed north of the Yinshan range in the _____ Dynasty.
   A) Han   B) Ming   C) Qin   D) Qing
4. The Great Wall is divided into _____ sections.
   A) four   B) five   C) three   D) two
5. There stand _____ major passes (Guan, in Chinese) at places of strategic importance along the Great Wall.

A) 14   B) 15   C) 20   D) 99

6. In 1987, the Wall was listed by UNESCO as a _____.

    A) scenic spot   B) wonder

    C) world cultural heritage site   D) place of interest

▶ *For questions 7-10, read the following statements, mark Y (for YES) if the statement agrees with the information given in the passage; N (for NO) if the statement contradicts the information given in the passage; NG (for NOT GIVEN) if the information is not given in the passage.*

_____ 7. The Wall climbs up and down, twists and turns along the ridges of the Yanshan and Yinshan Mountain Chains through six provinces, Beijing, Tianjin, and two autonomous regions.

_____ 8. Historical records trace the construction of the origin of the Wall to defensive fortification back to the year 565 B.C.

_____ 9. Most of Ming Dynasty Wall we see today was reinforced with bricks and rocks.

_____ 10. The Great Wall has been renovated every other year since the foundation of the PRC.

Passage Two

Three Scenic Spots in Hong Kong

1. Hong Kong Avenue of Stars

Hong Kong Avenue of Stars is located in Tsim Sha Tsui East (尖沙咀东部，尖东), Kowloon (九龙), Hong Kong's waterfront promenade (海滨长廊) in Tsim Sha Tsui waterfront park, opposite the New World Center with the Victoria Harbor connecting Tsim Sha Tsui East on the east and Hong Kong Museum of Art on the west. In 2003, New World Development Co., Ltd. spent 40 million Hong Kong dollars sponsoring on the construction of the Avenue of Stars, opening on April 27, 2004, and then transferred to the SAR Government (特别行政区政府) for public open space and tourists.

Avenue of Stars is an attraction built to pay tribute to the outstanding Hong Kong film industry people, following the Hollywood Walk of Fame with outstanding film workers' names and their palms embedded in commemorative plaques (匾) in order of age priority on the Avenue, and now the current capacity of Avenue of Stars holds 100 famous film workers in the commemorative plaques.

2. Tian Tan Buddha Statue (天坛大佛)

Tian Tan Buddha Statue, located in the Ngong Ping (昂坪) 520 meters above sea level, is a Buddha Statue on the Muyu Peak (木鱼峰顶), lying in front of the Po Lin Monastery (宝莲禅寺) on the Lantau Island (大屿山) in Hong Kong. Tian Tan Buddha, designed and built by the China Aerospace Science and Technology Department, sitting on the 268 stone steps, is made up of 202 copper components (Buddha 160, Lotus 36, cloud 6), with the height of 26.4 meters. If we take into account the Lotus Block and the total base, it is about 34 meters high and weighs 250 tones. It sits on the 3-layer altar, costing more than 60 million Hong Kong dollars, being the world's largest outdoor bronze Buddha block. The construction of the Tian Tan Buddha started in 1990, and the Buddha Statue itself was blessed on December 29, 1993 (November 17 Lunar New Year), the birthday of Amitabha Buddhist (阿弥陀佛), and it is now one of the famous tourist attractions in Hong Kong.

3. Victoria Harbor

Victoria Harbor is a harbor located between Hong Kong's Hong Kong Island and Kowloon Peninsula (九龙半岛). As a result of deep water port for natural harbor, Hong Kong has the reputation of "Pearl of the Orient", "the world's No. 3 major natural harbor" and "the world's No. 3 night scenic spot".

In earlier years, the British, seeing the Victoria Harbor as the East Asian region with an excellent potential for the port, did not hesitate to take the war from the hands of the government of Qing Dynasty and won the Hong Kong and the Far East to develop its maritime trade cause. Hong Kong's colonial history started immediately. In fact, the Victoria Harbor has indeed not only affected Hong Kong's history and culture, but also led Hong Kong's economic and tourism development, therefore it is one of the keys that makes Hong Kong an international city.

(545 words)

Exercises

For questions 1-6, read the following statements, mark Y (for YES) if the statement agrees with the information given in the passage; N (for NO) if the statement contradicts the information given in the passage; NG (for NOT GIVEN) if the information is not given in the passage.

_____ 1. Hong Kong Avenue of Stars was built in 2004, sponsored by New World Development Co., Ltd.

_____ 2. Avenue of Stars was built in honor of the outstanding pop stars in the HK show industry.

_____ 3. Opposite to the Avenue of Stars stands the New World Park.

_____ 4. The current capacity of Avenue of Stars is up to 100 famous film workers.

_____ 5. Tian Tan Buddha is the world's second largest outdoor bronze Buddha block.

_____ 6. Victoria Harbor is the world's No. 2 major natural harbor.

▶ *For questions 7-10, complete the sentences with the information given in the passage.*

7. Hong Kong Avenue of Stars is a _____.

8. Hong Kong has the reputation of "Pearl of the Orient".

9. _____ is one of the keys that makes Hong Kong an international city.

10. Hong Kong also has the reputation of "the world's _____ night scenic spot".

Section B

Passage One

Tips to Travelling in France

● If you're in a hurry you should be aware that the high speed TGV trains (高速列车) can transport you between several cities at more than 300kmh and often get you there faster than by air.

● Youth hostels provide about the cheapest holiday accommodation for single travelers enjoying a vacation in France on a tight budget. A dormitory bunk (铺位) can usually be booked for as little as US$20 per night.

● Plenty of motels can be found on most major routes and on the outskirts (郊区) of cities and towns, a bed alone costing as little as US$30 per night in 2004. Bed and breakfast accommodation is plentiful in even the most obscure locations and you can expect a room in a guesthouse to start from around US$270 per week.

● Long bus journeys can be slow but they are usually the cheapest way to travel so you can save a few dollars on your tickets during your holiday in France.

● However, a train pass such as Eurail (欧洲火车联票) can save even more dollars during your vacation in France if you intend covering a lot of territory.

● Holiday travel through France is very enjoyable by train on the country's 32,000 kilometers of rail line, about half of which is electrified.

● France has the most extensive rail network in Western Europe. The French domestic train service is among the fastest, most comfortable and efficient on the planet and is a great way to enjoy fairly cheap travel during your vacation in France.

● If you have enough money for the ticket, a TGV very fast train service connects the large cities at more than 300 kilometers per hour.

● Tourists from the UK should note that although the Eurostar train can very comfortably whisk you via (经过) the Eurotunnel[①] from central London to central Paris in less than three hours, the ticket price is much more than flying and the booking conditions on the train can be inconvenient.

● The domestic French bus and train network is integrated and your train ticket will in many cases also let you travel on a connecting bus.

● Various group and long distance return discounts are also available so it's worth closely studying the timetables and ticket packages before you head into the next step of your vacation in France.

● The quickest way to drive around France is on the autoroutes, although they're not particularly scenic (风景优美的). The speed limit in France is up to 130kmh.

● Autoroute toll fees are also expensive. For example, a 200-kilometer journey from La Rochelle (拉罗谢尔) to Bordeaux (波尔多) cost 11 euro (US$13.86) in 2005, and petrol prices are very high by international standards.

● It's cheaper to take the slower National Route (N) and Departmental (D) roads. It's smart to hire a small rather than a big car for your French vacation because many of the roads around country villages are cobblestone (鹅卵石) laneways (巷道) from centuries past and a small vehicle is easier to maneuver (操控).

● If you want to travel through France by car, beware that car rental rates and motorway tolls are expensive with traffic and parking problems in the cities that can make the whole exercise a waste of time and money.

● However, there are still plenty of well-maintained back roads criss-crossing the countryside—many with superb sightseeing—and you can cut the cost of private car travel if you're happy to avoid the motorways during your holiday through France.

● If you decide you want your own steering wheel, beware that French driving habits are fairly aggressive.

● Most villages and towns you drive through in the French countryside will have several prominent signs pointing to "chambres d'hotes", which is French for Bed and Breakfast. The average price for two in 2005 was US$102 per night. It's vital that you book ahead in the summer holiday months of July and August, when prices are generally higher.

● France has plenty of ferry and hovercraft (气垫船) links to England from ports such as Calais (加来), Boulogne (布伦), St-Malo (圣马洛), Roscoff (罗斯科夫), Brittany (布列塔尼) and Normandy (诺曼底).

● Numerous sea services can also be found for a voyage to Ireland, Italy, North Africa, Sardinia (撒丁岛) and the Channel Islands (海峡群岛).

● Most islands off the French coast can only be reached by ferry. It's worth booking your travel and holiday tickets ahead if possible.

● A cycling holiday in France is highly recommended as the country has an extensive network of cycle paths in both rural areas and cities.

● Uninsured bicycles can be rented for US$10-15 per day.

● If you base your France vacation in Paris or in most of the other major French cities, you'll find there's a fairly convenient metro network to whisk you around, running from 5:30 am to 1 am. Metro ticket prices in Paris are on a par (与……相当) with other cities.

● Budget for travel expenses around US$60 per day and you'll be able to find a comfortable private bed, adequate meals plus trips to tourist venues a few times a week. To travel in France on such a small budget, you'll probably need to buy your food in local markets rather than restaurants.

● It's possible to travel in France on survival rations costing as little as US$30 per day, and you'll be doing so little during your holiday that you may as well not be there.　　(998 words)

Note:

① 英吉利海峡隧道(the Channel Tunnel)，又称英法海底隧道或欧洲隧道(the Eurotunnel)，是一条连接英国英伦三岛与法国的铁路隧道，于 1994 年 5 月 6 日开通。该隧道由三条长 51 公里的平行隧洞组成，总长度 153 公里，其中海底段的单道隧洞长度为 38 公里。英、法、比利时三国铁路部门联营的"欧洲之星"(Eurostar)列车车速达每小时 300 公里。

Exercises

For questions 1-4, choose the best answer from the four choices marked A), B), C), and D) according to the information given in the passage.

1. According to the text, which one of the following is the cheapest when tourists travel in France?
   A) Long bus journeys.　　　　　　　　B) Cars.
   C) Trains.　　　　　　　　　　　　　D) Eurail.

2. Among the following lodging places, which one is the cheapest in France?
   A) Youth hostels.　　　　　　　　　　B) Motels.
   C) Guesthouses in obscure locations.　　D) Chambres d'hotes.

3. The French phrase "chambres d'hotes" on the prominent signs in the French countryside means that _____.
   A) there is a gas station nearby
   B) there is a restaurant nearby
   C) you can get accommodation nearby
   D) there is a police station nearby

4. Comprehensively speaking, which means of transportation is recommended for travel in France?
   A) Train.　　　B) Car.　　　C) Ferry.　　　D) Bicycle.

▶ *For questions 5-10, read the following statements, mark Y (for YES) if the statement agrees with the information given in the passage; N (for NO) if the statement contradicts the information given in the passage; NG (for NOT GIVEN) if the information is not given in the passage.*

_____ 5. In France the train tickets could only be used on the train proper.

_____ 6. All the train fees are cheaper than planes.

_____ 7. It's better to hire a small car because it is cheaper.

_____ 8. There are so many disadvantages of travelling by car in France that the tips try to dissuade people from using a car.

_____ 9. If you can only afford US$30 per day for travel, you are advised by the tips not to travel in France.

_____ 10. It can be inferred from the text that the quality of the trip hinges on one's budget.

Passage Two

A Fairyland—Pure New Zealand

I had my honeymoon in New Zealand. It was a nine-day self-driving tour. At first I thought we were crazy to have chosen New Zealand given the price of the whole budget. Besides, I was a bit apprehensive as it was my first time to go to an unfamiliar place without joining a tour package. However, the fear and anxiety were quickly dissolved by the marvelous scenery as well as the kindness and warmth of New Zealanders. When I finally visited the place, I simply fell in love with it. Heaven on the Earth, New Zealand is a nature lover's paradise. You don't need contrived amusement parks or fenced-off "scenic area". All you have to do is take a stroll and you can breathe, touch and see the beauty of this country. Wondrous scenery, pollution free, good climate, challenging activities...what more can one ask for?

No skyscraper in cities at all. A four or five-storied building is a high and huge one in South Island. Hence there is nothing to block the sight. I like the fact that walking outside and, even on the way to the grocery store, I can see the most breathtaking scenery all around me.

Secluded inlets (幽静的水湾), rugged snow-capped mountains, wild coast and picturesque (风景如画的) farming plains, all are like something that appears only in fairy tales. The West coast beaches attracted me most. Sitting on the black shimmering sand, listening to the wind singing, watching the fantastic tiding, we were exposed to a wild and pristine picture. It is really "heaven comes true"!

We could not help killing thirteen rolls of films during our stay. These photos allow us to relish our memories of New Zealand even till today. What else impresses us most is the efficient service system. We rent a car and drove throughout the South Island ourselves. There are several international car-rental companies like Herz, Avis and Budget in around the island. You can make a reservation through the Internet. It is quite convenient to get and return the car. We started our driving in Christchurch (基督城) and stopped in Dunedin (达尼丁) seven days later.

Fortunately we could find local Visitor Information Centers in most areas. In it there are maps and guide books and brochures of local events and entertainment, information of accommodation and restaurants, bulletins of attractions and activities, gifts, souvenirs, stamps and phone cards. Also friendly staffs with extensive local knowledge are available. They will answer any question you may have with patience, and provide advice regarding local attractions, travel, and accommodation requirements.

Most Visitor Information Centers can make reservations for accommodation, and may also be able to make direct bookings for travel, tours, accommodation and attractions. All the service is free. One lady there once helped us to book the motel in Arrowtown when there was no vacancy in Queenstown. We were charged only NZ$1.50 and that is the long-distance call fee. There was no extra spending at all.

This New Zealand Visitor Information Network (VIN) is an official one. Therefore, the information provided here is reliable. It is easy to recognize. Each center is identified by the distinctive logo and a green letter "I".

In the Dunedin Information Center we found a souvenir coin change machine. You can put all the left coins up to NZ$2; then it will give you a two-dollar New Zealand coin as a souvenir. Quite interesting! Simple-hearted New Zealanders call themselves Kiwi①. That is a special species existing merely on this island. The characteristics of it are simple and kind. That is just what a New Zealander has.

On the way, the cngine suddenly stalled. No matter how we tried, it just refused to work again. There was not even one car passing by. What should we do? Just then two bicycle-riding guys saw the parking car and came to us asking what was wrong. With their help, finally the car could move again.

Another time we lost the car key in Queenstown. When we realized it, we searched the way we walked inch by inch, hoping to find it, but failed. Then we were in panic for some time as all the things were in the car and what's more, the car number tag was on the key. We were a little released when we saw the car was still there. Then we just went to the Lost-and-Found to try our luck. The policeman was quite gentle and gave us all keys found within one hour to check. Our key was lying there! To find the key, we only spent about one hour including our own searching.

That is New Zealand. A simple but splendid place!   (796 words)

Note:

① 新西兰最早的移民毛利人根据几维鸟的叫声为其取名。这种不会飞的鸟，大小跟鸡差不多，有很长的嘴和毛发般的羽毛。新西兰人将这种可爱而不会飞的夜行鸟类作为新西兰的象征，定为国鸟，并将其形象使用在新西兰元硬币的正面。新西兰人常自豪地自称为 "Kiwi"，而很少称自己是 "New Zealander"。

Exercises

For questions1-5, complete the sentences with the information given in the passage.

1. My honeymoon in New Zealand was a nine-day _____ tour.

2. At first I was a bit _____ as it was my first time to go to an unfamiliar place without joining a tour package.

3. My fear and anxiety were quickly _____ by the marvelous scenery as well as the kindness and warmth of New Zealanders.

4. New Zealand is a nature lover's _____.

5. No _____ in cities at all.

▶ *For questions 6-10, choose the best explanation for the underlined word from the four choices marked A), B), C) and D) without changing the information given in the passage.*

6. You don't need <u>contrived</u> amusement parks or fenced-off "scenic areas".
   A. confused   B. bewildered
   C. refined   D. unnatural

7. <u>Wondrous</u> scenery, pollution free, good climate, challenging activities...what more can one ask for?
   A. spacious   B. sinistrous
   C. fantastic   D. antique

8. I can see the most <u>breathtaking</u> scenery all around me.
   A. inspiring   B. exciting
   C. heartbreaking   D. interesting

9. we were exposed to a wild and <u>pristine</u> picture
   A. original   B. excellent
   C. terrific   D. fabulous

10. On the way, the engine suddenly <u>stalled</u>.
    A. exhausted   B. halted
    C. distinguished   D. established

Unit Three

Lead-in

With one Disneyland park in Hong Kong and another one about to open in Shanghai, Disney is on its way to China. Different from the traditional view held about it, the Disneyland is not only for children alone but, in essence, for everyone that is young or young at heart. The magical land is always ready to give the full play to imaginations, fantasies and adventures. Most people touring there find themselves reemerge refreshed and revitalized. Despite the multiple benefits, Disney is also meeting problems when it is expanding globally. One of them is how to tailor its operational mode to the local taste. When the new Disney park opens in Shanghai, we hope, it can blend with the local culture.

 **Section A**

Passage One

A Brief Introduction to the Disneyland Park

Generally speaking, Disneyland parks are made up of four parts, namely, Main Street, U.S.A., Adventureland, Fantasyland and Tomorrowland. Let's take a brief look at them.

Main Street, U.S.A.

Main Street, U.S.A. is the first "themed land" inside the entrance of the many Magic Kingdom-style parks run by the Walt Disney Company around the world. Each Main Street, U.S.A. (except Tokyo Disneyland) has a train station above the entrance. At Disneyland, Disneyland Paris and Hong Kong Disneyland, Sleeping Beauty Castle stands in the distance beyond the end of the street. At the Magic Kingdom and Tokyo Disneyland, Cinderella Castle stands at the end.

Main Street, U.S.A. is the home to City Hall, in which the Guest Relations office is located. Further along Main Street, the names painted in the windows on Main Street serve as credits for some of the many people, Imagineers (幻想工程师) and others, who contributed in some way to the creation of Disneyland. Largely they appear as fictional businesses (gyms, realtors, dentists and the like), and they often refer to a hobby or interest that the person in question had. Ub Iwerks's[①] window, for example, refers to his prowess (高超技能) with cameras. For Disneyland's 50th anniversary, on July 17, 2005, a first-story window on each Main Street was unveiled (透露)

with a dedication to all the cast members (employees) who had worked for Disney throughout the years. The streets are paved with resilient (有弹性的) asphalt (沥青) to prevent aching of feet.

Adventureland

Adventureland is themed to resemble the remote jungles in Africa, Asia, the Middle East, desert islands, South America, and the South Pacific. "To create a land that would make this dream reality," said Walt Disney, "we pictured ourselves far from civilization, in the remote jungles of Asia and Africa."

Adventureland provides a 1950s view of exotic adventure, capitalizing on the post-war Tiki craze (风靡一时的事物)[2]. Lush vegetation resembles jungles while elements of the "other" surround the visitor. Tribal performance masks, Congo drums, non-American totem poles (图腾柱), exotic animal statues, and architecture of Pacific influence make for a confined area wherein industry and technology take a back seat to uncharted nature. Noted art historian David T. Doris explains Adventureland as, "a pastiche (模仿作品) of imaginary colonial spaces, conflated within the green and foliate (叶子状的) milieu (背景) of 'the Jungle'".

Fantasyland

Each Fantasyland has a castle as well as several gentle rides themed after Disney movies. In the words of Walt Disney: "Fantasyland is dedicated to the young at heart and to those who believe that when you wish upon a star, your dreams come true."

Tomorrowland

Each version of Tomorrowland is different and features numerous classic and unique attractions that depict (描绘) the numerous views of the future.

Walt Disney was known for his futurist views and showed the American public, through his television shows, how the world was moving into the future. Tomorrowland was the realized culmination (顶点) of his views. In his own words: "Tomorrow can be a wonderful age. Our scientists today are opening the doors of the Space Age to achievements that will benefit our children and generations to come. The Tomorrowland attractions have been designed to give you an opportunity to participate in adventures that are a living blueprint of our future."

Ironically, it is this movement into the future that has, on occasion, left Tomorrowland mired in the past. Disneyland's Tomorrowland is now in its third generation, and the Magic Kingdom's Tomorrowland is on its second. Disney itself has mentioned that it wanted to keep Tomorrowland from becoming "Yesterdayland". As a self-referential (自我指涉的) joke along this line, Disney's 2007 film *Meet the Robinsons* features an amusement park called "Todayland" that has rides that look remarkably like Space Mountain and Disneyland's original Rocket Jets.　　　　(680 words)

Note:

① Ub Iwerks（乌布·伊沃克斯）是华特·迪士尼在普雷斯曼鲁宾公司工作时的同事，后来两人合伙成立了伊沃克斯—迪士尼商业美术公司（Iwerks-Disney），由于从一项业务中总共才挣到 135 美元，伊沃克斯—迪士尼商业美术公司成立不到一个月就停业了。华特·迪士尼与哥哥创建迪士尼兄弟动画片制作公司后，再次招徕以前的合作伙伴乌布·伊沃克斯。伊沃克斯为迪士尼公司创造出了闻名全球的米老鼠形象。

② 夏威夷最早的居民大约 1,000 年前来自波利尼西亚，他们带来了自己的宗教信仰和神灵。夏威夷和波利尼西亚的许多神都是用图腾来表示的，Tiki 一词指的是整个波利尼西亚的神。从二十世纪三十年代开始，代表南太平洋岛屿生活的图腾文化开始形成，它以一些看上去古怪的雕像为代表。随着图腾文化的发展，具有南太平洋风格的图腾雕塑、图腾火炬、藤条编的家具、印有热带风光图案的衣服和木头或竹制品逐渐风靡。1959 年夏威夷成为美国的一个州以后，图腾文化、夏威夷衬衫和其他的夏威夷群岛的标志物成为了一种时尚。

Exercises

For questions 1-6, there are three definitions below each underlined word in the passage. One definition is closest to its meaning. One definition has the opposite or nearly opposite meaning. The remaining definition has a completely different meaning. Label the definitions C for closest, O for opposite, and D for different.

1. Further along Main Street, the names painted in the windows on Main Street serve as <u>credits</u> for some of the many people, Imagineers and others, who contributed in some way to the creation of Disneyland.
   - _____ A) payment
   - _____ B) recognition
   - _____ C) disapproval

2. Adventureland provides a 1950s view of <u>exotic</u> adventure, capitalizing on the post-war Tiki craze.
   - _____ A) foreign
   - _____ B) domestic
   - _____ C) exquisite

3. <u>Lush</u> vegetation resembles jungles while elements of the "other" surround the visitor.
   - _____ A) sparse
   - _____ B) luxurious
   - _____ C) laxuriant

4. Tribal performance masks, Congo drums, non-American totem poles, exotic animal statues, and architecture of Pacific influence make for a <u>confined</u> area wherein industry and technology take a back seat to uncharted nature.
   - _____ A) boundless
   - _____ B) intensive
   - _____ C) enclosed

5. Tribal performance masks, Congo drums, non-American totem poles, exotic animal statues, and architecture of Pacific influence make for a confined area wherein industry and technology take a back seat to <u>uncharted</u> nature.
   - _____ A) little-known
   - _____ B) well-known
   - _____ C) best-known

6. Ironically, it is this movement into the future that has, on occasion, left Tomorrowland <u>mired</u> in the past.

      _____ A) stalemated

      _____ B) mocked

      _____ C) stuck

▶ *For questions 7-10, complete the sentences with the information given in the passage.*

7. Disneyland parks are usually made up of _____, _____, _____ and _____.

8. In Tokyo Disneyland, _____ stands at the end of the Main Street, U.S.A.

9. According to Walt Disney, Fantasyland is dedicated to _____.

10. Each version of Tomorrowland features _____ that depict _____.

Passage Two

Incidents at Disney Parks

This is a summary of notable incidents that have taken place at various Disney-owned theme parks, amusement parks, or water parks.

The term incidents refer to major accidents, injuries, deaths, or significant crimes that occur at a Disney park. While these incidents were required to be reported to regulatory authorities for investigation, attraction-related incidents usually fall into one of the following categories:

1. The incident caused by negligence on the part of the guest can be refusal to follow specific ride safety instructions, or deliberate intent to break park rules.

2. The incident result of guests' known or unknown health issues.

3. The incident caused by negligence on the part of the park, either by ride operator or by maintenance.

4. Act of God or a generic accident (e.g. slipping and falling), that is not a direct result of an action on anybody's part.

In 1964, 15-year-old Mark Maples of Long Beach, California, was injured after he stood up in the Matterhorn Bobsleds and fell out. It is reported that his restraint was undone by his ride companion. He died three days later as a result of these injuries.

On July 8, 1974, employee Deborah Gail Stone, 18, of Santa Ana, California was crushed to death between a revolving wall and a stationary platform inside the America Sings attraction. She was in the wrong place during a ride intermission; it was unclear whether this was due to inadequate training or a misstep. The attraction was subsequently refitted with breakaway walls.

On January 3, 1984, 48-year-old Dolly Regina Young of Fremont, California was killed when she was thrown from a Matterhorn Bobsleds car and struck by the next oncoming bobsled (雪橇). An investigation showed that her seatbelt was found unbuckled after the accident. It is still unclear whether Young deliberately unfastened her belt or if the seatbelt malfunctioned.

On February 14, 1999, 65-year-old part-time custodian (看守人) Raymond Barlow was mortally injured when he fell off the Skyway ride. He was cleaning the Fantasyland Skyway station platform when the ride was accidentally turned on. Barlow was in the path of the ride vehicles, and grabbed a passing gondola (车厢) in an attempt to save himself. He lost his grip and fell 40 feet, landing in a flower bed near the Dumbo ride. He died shortly after being taken to a local hospital. The Skyway ride, which had been scheduled to be closed before the accident occurred, was permanently closed on November 10, 1999. As a result of the accident, Walt Disney World paid the family of the man US$2,500,000 in compensation.

On June 25, 2000, 23-year-old Cristina Moreno of Barcelona, Spain, exited the Indiana Jones ride complaining of a severe headache. She was hospitalized later that day where it was discovered that she had brain hemorrhaging (出血). She died on September 1, 2000, of a brain aneurysm (动脉瘤). Her family's subsequent wrongful death lawsuit against Disney stated that Moreno died due to "violent shaking and stresses imposed by the ride". In an interlocutory appeal (非正式上诉), the California Supreme Court held that amusement parks are considered "common carriers" similar to commercially operated planes, trains, elevators, and ski lifts. This ruling imposes a heightened duty of care on amusement parks and requires them to provide the same degree of care and safety as other common carriers. Disney settled the lawsuit for an undisclosed sum after the interlocutory appeal but before a decision was rendered on the case's merits. Moreno's medical costs were estimated at more than US$1.3 million.

On September 5, 2003, 22-year-old Marcelo Torres of nearby Gardena, California died after suffering severe blunt force trauma (损伤) and extensive internal bleeding in a derailment (出轨) of the Big Thunder Mountain Railroad roller coaster that also injured 11 other riders. The cause of the accident was determined to be improper maintenance and training of Disney employees. Investigation reports and discovery by Torres' attorney confirmed Mr. Torres' fatal injuries occurred when the first passenger car collided with the underside of the locomotive. The derailment was in part the result of a mechanical failure, which occurred as a result of, among other things, omissions during a maintenance procedure of at least two required actions, the left side upstop/guide wheel on the floating axle of the locomotive was not tightened in accordance with specifications; and a safety wire was not installed or completed the necessary maintenance required by said tagging system, all with knowledge of Disney management and personnel. The theme park settled a lawsuit with the victim and the survivors for $25,000,000.

77-year-old Gloria Land of Minnesota lost consciousness and died after riding in February 2005. A medical examiner's report said Land was in poor health from diabetes (糖尿病) and she previously had several mini strokes. The report concluded that her death "was not unexpected".

6-year-old Rame Masarwa fainted after riding Space Mountain on August 1, 2006, and was taken to Florida Hospital Celebration where he later died. The medical examiner's report showed that Masarwa, who was terminally ill and suffered from cancer of the lungs, spine, and abdomen, died of natural causes due to a metastatic pulmonary blastoma tumor (肺部孤立性转移肿瘤). Masarwa was visiting the Magic Kingdom as a recipient of a trip by the Give Kids the World program.

On December 7, 2006, 73-year-old Michael Chartrand lost consciousness while riding Space Mountain. After being taken to the hospital, he died three days later. The medical examiner's report stated that the man died of natural causes due to a heart condition.   (957 words)

Exercises

For questions 1-6, choose the best answer from the four choices marked A), B), C) and D) according to the information given in the passage.

1. Cristina Moreno died because of _____.
   A) her own misstep   B) poor maintenance
   C) poor health   D) brain hemorrhaging
2. The cause of Dolly Regina Young's death is _____.
   A) the unfastened belt   B) diabetes
   C) a false step   D) not known
3. Raymond Barlow's death was caused by _____.
   A) accidental running of the ride   B) his negligence
   C) his belt being undone   D) a stroke
4. Which of the following accidents is not blamed on the park?
   A) Raymond Barlow's death.   B) Cristina Moreno's death.
   C) Mark Maples' death.   D) Marcelo Torres' death.
5. Which one of them didn't die of their own poor health?
   A) Rame Masarwa.   B) Dolly Regina Young.
   C) Gloria Land.   D) Michael Chartrand.
6. Which of the following cases didn't involve monetary compensation?
   A) Marcelo Torres' death.   B) Cristina Moreno's death.
   C) Gloria Land's death.   D) Raymond Barlow's death.

▶ ***For questions 7-10, there are three definitions below each underlined word in the passage. One definition is closest to its meaning. One definition has the opposite or nearly opposite meaning. The remaining definition has a completely different meaning. Label the definitions C for closest, O for opposite, and D for different.***

7. The incident caused by <u>negligence</u> on the part of the park, either by ride operator or by maintenance.
   _____ A) prudence
   _____ B) patience
   _____ C) carelessness

8. On July 8, 1974, employee Deborah Gail Stone, 18, of Santa Ana, California was crushed to death between a revolving wall and a <u>stationary</u> platform inside the America Sings attraction.

   _____ A) moving

   _____ B) stationery

   _____ C) still

9. On February 14, 1999, 65-year-old part-time custodian Raymond Barlow was <u>mortally</u> injured when he fell off the Skyway ride.

   _____ A) toughly

   _____ B) fatally

   _____ C) slightly

10. The Skyway ride, which had been scheduled to be closed before the accident occurred, was <u>permanently</u> closed on November 10, 1999.

   _____ A) for fun

   _____ B) for the time being

   _____ C) for good

Section B

Passage One

Hong Kong Disneyland Park

To all who come to this happy place, welcome! Many years ago, Walt Disney introduced the world to enchanted realms (王国) of fantasy and adventure, yesterday and tomorrow, in a magical place called Disneyland. Today that spirit of imagination and discovery comes to life in Hong Kong.

Hong Kong Disneyland is dedicated to the young and the young at heart—with the hope that it will be a source of joy and inspiration, and an enduring symbol of the cooperation, friendship and understanding between the people of Hong Kong and the United States of America.

—Michael D. Eisner and Donald Tsang, September 12, 2005 (Grand Opening)

An audience of more than 400 guests celebrated the ground breaking of Hong Kong Disneyland on January 12, 2003. Those present included Tung Chee Hwa, then Chief Executive of the Hong Kong Special Administrative Region of the People's Republic of China; Michael D. Eisner, Chairman and CEO of The Walt Disney Company; and Robert A. Iger, President of The Walt Disney Company.

On September 23, 2004, a special "castle topping ceremony" was held in the park to commemorate (庆祝) the placing of the tallest turret (小塔楼) on Sleeping Beauty Castle. Among those present were Tung Chee Hwa, then Chief Executive of the Hong Kong Special Administrative Region of the People's Republic of China; Jay Rasulo, president of Walt Disney Parks and Resorts; Michael Eisner, then CEO of The Walt Disney Company; and Bob Iger, president of The Walt Disney Company, in addition to Mickey Mouse and other costumed characters. Hong Kong Disneyland had the shortest construction period among all of the Disneyland-style theme parks.

Hong Kong Disneyland is the first theme park inside the Hong Kong Disneyland Resort and is owned and managed by the Hong Kong International Theme Parks, an incorporated company jointly owned by The Walt Disney Company and the government of Hong Kong.

The fifth Disneyland style park is located on reclaimed land in Penny's Bay (竹蒿湾), Lantau Island (大屿山). After years of negotiations and construction, the park opened to visitors on September 12, 2005, considered an auspicious (吉祥的) date according to Chinese almanacs (历书) for the opening of a new business. Disney attempted to avoid problems of cultural backlash (对抗) by attempting to incorporate Chinese culture, customs, and traditions when designing and building the resort.

The park consists of four themed lands similar to other Disneyland parks: Main Street, U.S.A., Fantasyland, Adventureland and Tomorrowland. There is as yet no Frontierland, although it may be included in future expansion projects. The theme park's cast members use English and Chinese, including Cantonese and Mandarin dialects, to communicate verbally (口头地). Guide maps are printed in both Traditional and Simplified characters, Japanese, and in English.

The capacity of the park is 34,000 visitors per day, and is the smallest Disneyland Park. It has so far fallen short of meeting its targeted visitor-ship figures. The park attracted 5.2 million visitors in its first year, below its target of 5.6 million. Visitor numbers fell 20% in the second year to 4 million, which was below company targets, inciting criticisms from local legislators (议员).

The resort currently has 310 acres (1.3 km^2), with the actual park taking approximately 100 acres (0.4 km^2). With its small size cited often to explain its under-performance, the park has announced various plans for expansion. The classic Disney attraction, "it's a small world", opened on 28 April 2008. Furthermore, according to Bill Ernest, the former executive vice president and managing director of Hong Kong Disneyland, the park is planning to add two unique theme lands in its future expansion. Over a 15-year expansion period, the park capacity will increase to handle up to 10 million visitors annually.   (650 words)

Exercises

For questions 1-7, read the following statements, mark Y (for YES) if the statement agrees with the information given in the passage; N (for NO) if the statement contradicts the information given in the passage; NG (for NOT GIVEN) if the information is not given in the passage.

_____ 1. The park opened on September 12, 2005, a date considered to be favorable for the opening of a new business.

_____ 2. Hong Kong Disneyland Park consists of Main Street, U.S.A., Fantasyland, Adventureland, Tomorrowland and Frontierland.

_____ 3. Hong Kong Disneyland Park has had the shortest construction period and by far is the largest of its kind in the world.

_____ 4. The trend of the decrease in tourist numbers will be reversed in no time.

_____ 5. According to the released figures, the park saw a steady year-on-year growth of visitor numbers.

_____ 6. According to the former executive vice president and managing director of Hong Kong Disneyland, the park will consist of six theme lands in the future.

_____ 7. The park capacity is expected to be nearly doubled on that of the present.

▶ *For questions 8-10, complete the sentences with the information given in the passage.*

8. According to Paragraph 1, Walt Disney introduced the world to _____ in Disneyland.

9. In Hong Kong, Disney tried to solve cultural differences between the east and the west by _____ when designing and building the resort.

10. The gap between the visitor number and the targeted visitor-ship number is _____ (how many).

Passage Two

Disney's Hong Kong Headache

Hong Kong's Magic Kingdom has so far been a little short on magic. Disney executives touted (吹嘘) the $1.8 billion theme park as its biggest, boldest effort to build its brand in China, a potentially vast new market for its toys, DVDs and movies. The Hong Kong government, which aggressively wooed (努力说服) Disney and is the park's majority owner hoped Disneyland would help secure (促成) the city's reputation as one of Asia's top tourist destinations. However, the conservative approach of Disney and its partner have produced a pint-sized park that so far hasn't matched visitors' lofty expectations. Hong Kong Disneyland has a mere 16 attractions? Only a classic Disney thrill ride, Space Mountain, compared to 52 at Disneyland Resort Paris. Meanwhile, management glitches involving everything from ticketing to employee relations have further tarnished the venture's image. In a recent survey conducted by Hong Kong Polytechnic University (香港理工大学), 70% of the local residents polled said they had a more negative opinion of Disneyland since its opening. "Disney knows the theme-park business, but when it comes to understanding the Chinese guest, it's an entirely new ball game," says John Ap, an associate professor at the university's School of Hotel and Tourism Management.

Nonetheless, Disney executives insist the park is on track (进展顺利). Jay Rasulo, chairman of

Walt Disney Parks and Resorts, says, "I feel great about how Hong Kong Disneyland is doing." Disney's own surveys of park visitors show an 80% satisfaction rate, among the highest of any of the company's parks. Rasulo says, "People feel this is a great experience."

The Burbank, California, headquartered company knows what it is talking about; it welcomed its two billionth visitor last week. And it is no stranger to tempestuous (风云变幻的) beginnings at an international park, at times caused by imposing a very American sensibility on foreign guests. When Disneyland Paris opened in 1992, Disney famously banned wine from park restaurants, much to the dismay of European bons vivants ([法]讲究饮食和社交的人). In Hong Kong, Disney went out of its way to tailor the park to local tastes. Its Imagineers installed Main Street's first Chinese eatery (餐馆), along with Fantasy Gardens where Mickey Mouse, local favorite Mulan and other Disney characters reside so tourists can readily snap pictures with them. Ironically, Disney's most high-profile stumble resulted from being too local. When executives decided to serve shark-fin soup, a Hong Kong favorite, environmentalists howled and Disney ignominiously (丢脸地) yanked it from the menu.

Another embarrassment came over the Lunar New Year holiday beginning in January, a popular vacation time in China. Disney neglected to block off the entire week as "special days" for which visitors required specific tickets. Tourists with valid tickets got turned away at the front gates after the park quickly filled up; the jilted (被抛弃的) travelers screamed at park employees, while TV cameras filmed one family trying to pass a child over the fence. Henry Tang, the city's Financial Secretary, voiced concern that this disarray (混乱) "might affect the image of Hong Kong's tourism industry". Bill Ernest, Hong Kong Disneyland's managing director, says the company "had no idea" that demand would spike so sharply at that time and adds that Disney has since expanded the number of "special days" to improve crowd control during holidays, "We don't make the same mistake twice."

Some workers assigned to play the parts of supposedly cheery characters like Mickey and Tigger have also complained. In April, the Hong Kong Disneyland Cast Members' Union made public a litany of gripes over poor pay, excessive work hours and, most of all, the sweltering conditions inside their costumes. Disney counters that the complaints are an "inaccurate representation" of the work environment at the park, that staffers have been granted extra rest days beyond those mandated (授权) by their contracts, and that their costumes are no different to those worn at its hot park in Florida.

"Given the complexity of the Hong Kong operation, such "teething pains" are hardly surprising," says Rasulo. What may be tougher to solve, though, are the yawns the miniature park is generating among tourists. Rasulo says the park wasn't built on a grand scale because the Chinese didn't grow up with Disney and don't know the characters as well as Americans and Europeans do, which acts as a constraint on its potential audience. Ernest calls it a "great introductory park". They also point out that the company plans to keep adding new attractions at Hong Kong Disneyland, including an updated version of Disney's classic Autopia racing game, scheduled to open this summer. The government is reclaiming land on an adjoining site to expand the park further. But James Zoltak, editor of *Amusement Business*, a trade magazine for the theme-park industry, says Disney isn't moving quickly enough: It needs to "get on a crash course in terms of expansion. The rate of building it up has to be swifter than anything they've done at any of their parks".

"Disney continues to bet that its long-range investment plans in China will pay off, regardless of the recent headaches in Hong Kong. The firm is still in talks with Chinese officials about opening a mainland theme park, possibly in Shanghai," says Rasulo. "Have we made some mistakes?" he asks. "Absolutely. We are in a brand-new market. We have to keep listening and keep learning." Restoring Tinkerbell's health only requires a round of applause, but Hong Kong Disneyland will need a bit more work. (961 words)

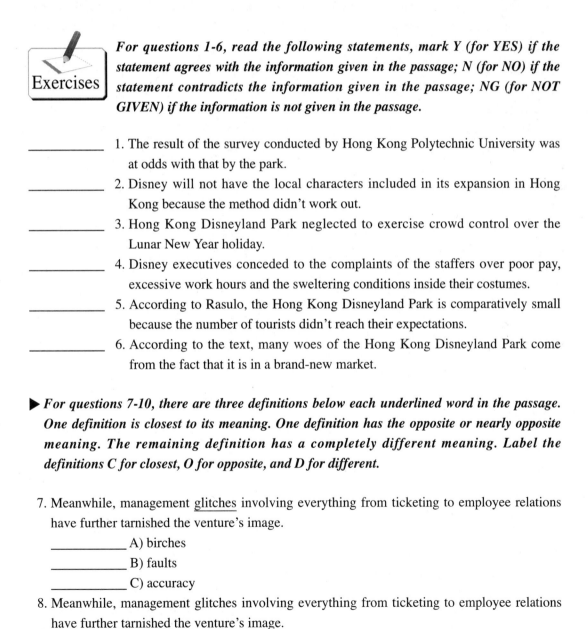

Exercises

For questions 1-6, read the following statements, mark Y (for YES) if the statement agrees with the information given in the passage; N (for NO) if the statement contradicts the information given in the passage; NG (for NOT GIVEN) if the information is not given in the passage.

_____ 1. The result of the survey conducted by Hong Kong Polytechnic University was at odds with that by the park.

_____ 2. Disney will not have the local characters included in its expansion in Hong Kong because the method didn't work out.

_____ 3. Hong Kong Disneyland Park neglected to exercise crowd control over the Lunar New Year holiday.

_____ 4. Disney executives conceded to the complaints of the staffers over poor pay, excessive work hours and the sweltering conditions inside their costumes.

_____ 5. According to Rasulo, the Hong Kong Disneyland Park is comparatively small because the number of tourists didn't reach their expectations.

_____ 6. According to the text, many woes of the Hong Kong Disneyland Park come from the fact that it is in a brand-new market.

▶ *For questions 7-10, there are three definitions below each underlined word in the passage. One definition is closest to its meaning. One definition has the opposite or nearly opposite meaning. The remaining definition has a completely different meaning. Label the definitions C for closest, O for opposite, and D for different.*

7. Meanwhile, management <u>glitches</u> involving everything from ticketing to employee relations have further tarnished the venture's image.

_____ A) birches

_____ B) faults

_____ C) accuracy

8. Meanwhile, management glitches involving everything from ticketing to employee relations have further <u>tarnished</u> the venture's image.

_____ A) burnished

_____ B) tickled

_____ C) stained

9. Bill Ernest, Hong Kong Disneyland's managing director, says the company "had no idea" that demand would <u>spike</u> so sharply at that time and adds that Disney has since expanded the number of "special days" to improve crowd control during holidays, "We don't make the same mistake twice."

_____ A) drop

_____ B) increase

_____ C) spade

10. In April, the Hong Kong Disneyland Cast Members' Union made public a litany of <u>gripes</u> over poor pay, excessive work hours and, most of all, the sweltering conditions inside their costumes.

_____ A) grapes

_____ B) contentment

_____ C) complaints

Unit Four

Lead-in

Teachers, the human soul engineers, play a vital role in students' all-round development. They serve not only as students' instructors but also their friends and facilitators. Peking opera, today, has been brought into classrooms in an effort to carry on the traditional culture and shape students' character comprehensively. However, there are still problems. Corporal punishment, arguably the legacy of Confucius, is still deep-rooted in the mind of many teachers and, with China going global, the conventional learning by rote is lagging further and further behind the multinational's demand for the creative talents with the teamwork awareness. How to tackle the problems is becoming an urgent issue for the Chinese government.

 **Section A**

Passage One

Mentors, Not Tormentors

When Sui Yue landed a job at her alma mater (母校) after graduating from university, she first visited her former high school's head teacher, to seek advice on how to get along with students.

"Well, you can either try to become their best friend, or be strict and distant, someone the students fear," the teacher told her.

Sui chose to be the former—an amiable and approachable teacher. Although five years have passed, she still has difficulty truly understanding her teenage students, with whom she spends most of the day.

"A teacher's work is pretty tiring and challenging nowadays, because we are facing a much more demanding generation of students," says Sui. She teaches English and is also in charge of a sophomore class of 56 at the No. 4 High School in Shenyang, capital of Liaoning Province.

She remembers a more simple teacher-and-student relationship when she attended high school a decade ago. Teenagers then were not exposed to the Internet and tended to be innocent and like-minded.

"We revered our teachers and put them on a pedestal," she says.

"Today's post-'90s generation of students are faced with an information overload," says Sui. They have independent opinions and have forged their own unique personalities.

With the emergence of different social classes, she also notes a growing information gap between students from low-income and high-income families. While some students can afford the latest mobile phone that can connect to the Internet, their less well-off peers may not even have a basic one.

"Such an imbalance results in some students adopting a pessimistic attitude toward everything, and this renders the task of the teacher even more complex and difficult," says Sui.

While Liu Hong does not have to face a class of agitated teens like Sui does, her much younger students pose no less of a challenge. Liu, 33, a primary school teacher in Shenyang, has been teaching for 14 years, and has been head teacher for 10 years. She says she is often confused by what goes on in students' minds these days.

"They are smart and precocious. They are well aware of what is happening outside, thanks to the rapid advancements in technology and widespread use of the Internet," she says, adding that she is often baffled by their questions and riddles picked up online.

Liu says that most of her students are quite self-centered. She recalls a boy in her class who would be dejected for the whole day if others as much as touched his belongings.

Sui says that since children usually grow up in a tolerant home environment, they are sometimes overly sensitive to well-intentioned criticism. Another head teacher of her grade once tried to motivate a girl by expressing a little disapproval over her performance. The girl could not accept it and cried for days.

The old adage that "strict teachers produce outstanding students", she says, no longer holds true.

"Nowadays, a single method of education cannot meet the needs of all students. Teachers need to adopt a more comprehensive evaluation system and a differentiated approach to teaching," she says.

Liu Xiaolin, whose fourth-grade son attends a school in Beijing, says that teachers today are under huge pressure, and this can partly be attributed to the high expectations of parents.

"The new generation parents are young and well-educated, and because they have only one child, they pay much more attention to their child's performance in school," she says.

She says parents have become more demanding of teachers and expect equal care and treatment of students. After every parent-teacher meeting, she says, she always sees groups of parents crowding around teachers and throwing questions at them.

Last month, the Ministry of Education put forth its "Regulations for Head Teachers of Primary and Middle Schools", and one article approves teachers' right to criticize and deal with recalcitrant students in an appropriate manner. This provision has fueled considerable debate over whether criticism is part of a teacher's duties. Explaining its inclusion, an official from the ministry said that some head teachers dared not correct students for fear of incurring their parents' wrath.

Commenting on the recent spate of media coverage of spats (小争吵) between teachers and students, Liu Hong says many of them are biased. She complains that some reporters only listen to the parents while turning a deaf ear to teachers. She believes that while criticism is necessary, teachers are being encouraged to shower more praise on students than in the past.

"We have a mobile message service network connecting our school and parents. I send two or three messages a day to parents, reporting on the homework, children's performance and the latest events at school," she says.

Sui Yue says that it is natural that sometimes parents will misunderstand teachers, because they have transferred their hopes for their children onto the teachers.

"I think criticism is always the last choice for teachers."

"Students change, yet love is always the center of all education." (833 words)

Exercises

For questions 1-10, complete the sentences with the information given in the passage.

1. When Sui Yue _____ a job at her alma mater after graduating from university, she first visited her former high school's head teacher, to seek advice on how to get along with students.
2. Sui chose to be the former—an _____ and _____ teacher.
3. Teachers are facing a much more _____ generation of students.
4. Teachers today are under huge pressure, and this can partly be attributed to the high _____ of parents.
5. Teenagers then were not exposed to the Internet and tended to be innocent and _____.
6. She recalls a boy in her class who would be _____ for the whole day if others as much as touched his belongings.
7. Teachers are entitled to criticize and deal with _____ students in an appropriate manner.
8. Students today are well aware of what is happening outside, thanks to the rapid _____ in technology and widespread use of the Internet.
9. The old _____ that "strict teachers produce outstanding students", she says, no longer holds true.
10. Students change, yet _____ is always the center of all education.

Passage Two

Let Kids Rest Their Eyes in Open Country

On Monday, most Chinese newspapers and news websites carried a photograph of Premier Wen Jiabao sitting in a classroom in a high school in Beijing, listening attentively to the teacher and noting down what the teacher said.

While I was moved because of the concern shown by the government leader for the education of our younger generation, I was somewhat worried over what I saw in the picture.

Of the five boys sitting in the front rows before the premier, four were wearing glasses. They were bent over their desks writing with their eyes just a few inches from the notebooks. I couldn't help worrying that their eyesight would worsen soon.

Ironically, the 67-year-old premier sat with his back perfectly straight—in a standard posture as is required in the Basic Knowledge and Requirements for the Protection of Eyesight of Primary and Middle School Students, issued by the Ministry of Education.

Shortsightedness is alarmingly serious among Chinese students. A recent survey shows the incidence of myopia (近视) is 22.78 percent among primary school pupils, and 55.22 percent and a whopping 76.74 percent among high school and college students. Myopia-related cases among all Chinese youths has reached a high of 60 percent, second only to that in Japan, according to the latest survey, conducted jointly by the Ministry of Education and Ministry of Health. Twenty years ago, it was only about 30 percent.

What is more worrisome is that cases have been growing at an annual rate of 5 percent in recent years.

If this situation continues, the quality of our future workforce will deteriorate so much that our nation's development will be seriously impaired.

In fact, there are already signs of such deterioration. Some marine navigation colleges have reportedly had to lower the floor marks for enrollment to meet the requirement on eyesight. But still many students with high marks were disqualified because of myopia.

The phenomenon is the result of too heavy a burden of study, imposed by teachers and parents, on youngsters. Given the current trend—the teachers' aspiration for higher performance assessment and the parents' eagerness to see their children's "academic attainment", it seems unrealistic that the burden will be reduced significantly any time soon. But we could do at least one thing: reflect on, and correct, the way we let our kids spend their spare time.

Ophthalmologists (眼科医师) tell us that the crystalline lens and ciliary muscle (睫状肌) of a youth's eyes have a strong ability for self-recovery as long as proper methods are adopted to reduce the tension on the eyes caused by hard work. Looking into the distance, especially during outdoor activities, is the best way to let our eyes rest.

Chinese students, however, hardly perform many outdoor activities. Most of their pastime is spent playing video games or watching TV, which their parents allow as a reward for their "hard study". Their eyes hardly get any rest.

When I was a child, we students played outdoor games after school and often went to the outskirts to catch fish and insects for fun. Every summer vacation, my parents sent me to my grandparents in the countryside. It was a great relief from my school studies.

A very small percentage of students of my time suffered from myopia, though unfortunately I developed shortsightedness after I entered senior high school.

Schools and education authorities should take resolute measures to increase outdoor activities for youngsters. Summer and winter vacations are especially important for students to get a respite (放松) from their hard work of several months.

I hope there is a law to ban all academic work for students during vacations. The idea may sound too radical. But I believe in the old saying: Overcorrecting is necessary in righting a wrong. It is necessary for any corrective measure in today's China. (649 words)

Exercises

For questions 1-6 complete the sentences with the information given in the passage.

1. While I was _____ because of the concern shown by the government leader for the education of our younger generation, I was somewhat worried over what I saw in the picture.
2. I couldn't help worrying that their eyesight would _____ soon.
3. Ironically, the _____ premier sat with his back perfectly straight—in a standard posture as is required in the Basic Knowledge and Requirements for the Protection of Eyesight of Primary and Middle School Students, issued by the Ministry of Education.
4. If this situation continues, the quality of our future workforce will _____ so much that our nation's development will be seriously impaired.
5. Some marine navigation colleges have reportedly had to lower the _____ marks for enrollment to meet the requirement on eyesight.
6. Most of their _____ is spent playing video games or watching TV.

▶ *For questions 7-10, read the following statements, mark Y (for YES) if the statement agrees with the information given in the passage; N (for NO) if the statement contradicts the information given in the passage; NG (for NOT GIVEN) if the information is not given in the passage.*

_____ 7. What is more worrisome is that cases have been growing at an annual rate of 6 percent in recent years.
_____ 8. The phenomenon is the result of too heavy a burden of study, imposed by their friends, on youngsters.
_____ 9. The students' burden will become lighter and lighter as they grow up.
_____ 10. Summer and winter vacations are especially important for students to get a respite (放松) from their hard work of several months.

Passage One

Beijing Students to Learn Peking Opera

Students in Beijing's schools found their grandfathers' favorite Peking Opera pieces (作品) in their music class repertoire (全部曲目) as the new semester began on Monday.

"I am expecting my first music class to learn Peking Opera and I expect to wear the fancy facial makeup," said Zhang Yaoyin, a third grade student in Beijing No. 2 Experimental Primary School on her way to the school.

Peking Opera was added into music courses in 20 Beijing primary and secondary schools in order to promote traditional Chinese culture.

"Peking Opera is very vivid and I like the melody best," she said, wondering whether her school had been chosen as a pilot.

Zhang Suhan, her father, called the action a "must" in the preservation and revitalization (复兴) of Chinese culture.

Some parents voiced concern about the new content of the music classes and the impact on students' chances for university admission.

"The action, which seems well-intentioned, will backfire and impose more burdens on children, because it is the exam scores that count when you apply for a good university in China," said a parent surnamed Zhang, who was waiting outside a school to pick up his son.

His son already takes several "interest classes", including piano, art and English. "I do not want Peking Opera to take up his time," he added.

Peking Opera, known as China's national opera, is facing the danger of extinction as the younger generation prefers pop culture to its slow pace and abstruse (难理解的) lyrics.

The Ministry of Education decided this month to start a pilot project in the new semester in 200 schools in 10 provinces, autonomous regions (自治区) and municipalities (直辖市).

The project added 15 pieces of Peking Opera, both classical and modern, into music courses.

Music teachers in Beijing schools were required to learn how to perform Peking Opera before introducing it to their students.

"Teachers play a critical role in introducing Peking Opera to students and making them like it," said Wu Jiang, an official with the Education Ministry.

"Most teachers themselves do not know how to perform the almost forgotten art form," said a principal in Beijing's Dongcheng District.

"It is the basic requirement that every music teacher in Beijing should be able to sing Peking Opera," said Wang Jun, a local education official.

The news, however, has aroused great controversy. In a survey by Netease, a news portal in

China, nearly 70 percent of respondents ([民意调查的] 调查对象) were against the project.

"It is good to introduce traditional culture to students, but specific situations in different parts of China should be taken into consideration," said Yuan Li, a professional researcher with the China Institute of Art.

"It may be good for Beijing kids to learn Peking Opera, but is it fit for a Tong kid in the remote Guizhou Province?" said Yuan.

The opera, with a history of more than 200 years, is a synthesis (综合体) of music, dance, art and acrobatics and is widely regarded as a symbolic expression of Chinese culture.

Many historical events have been adapted into the plays, which in the past were an important primer (入门指南) on history and ethical principles.   (567 words)

Exercises

For questions 1-5, complete the sentences with the information given in the passage.

1. Zhang Yaoyin was eager to learn Peking Opera, because _____.
2. Peking Opera is an almost forgotten art form; it is on the brink of _____.
3. Peking Opera has a history of more than _____ years; it integrates_____, _____, _____ and _____; it is widely regarded as _____.
4. According to the interviewed parent, _____ counts when students apply for a good university in China.
5. Peking Opera in the past served as an important primer on _____.

▶ *For questions 6-10, read the following statements, mark Y (for YES) if the statement agrees with the information given in the passage; N (for NO) if the statement contradicts the information given in the passage; NG (for NOT GIVEN) if the information is not given in the passage.*

_____ 6. The project of adding Peking Opera is planned as a test or a trial by the Ministry of Education.

_____ 7. Peking Opera is a very old art form, so only classical pieces will be introduced to the students.

_____ 8. There are a number of teachers who can perform Peking Opera, and it is they who are trying to preserve this kind of art form by introducing it to their students.

_____ 9. It can be inferred from the text that Peking Opera will become a "must" in a school's curricula.

_____ 10. The author is negative and disapproving towards this project.

Bilingual Education in the United States

Bilingual education is an educational program that provides instruction in both the student's native language and the language of the host country. In the United States, bilingual programs give instruction in English and some other language, such as Spanish or Vietnamese.

Bilingual education became federal law in 1974. According to the Bilingual Education Act of 1974, public schools must provide equal educational opportunities for students who speak languages other than English. This law recommended that federal money be given to states so that they could implement bilingual programs and teacher training, classes in students' native language, and English as a Second Language (ESL).

Some states had begun their own bilingual programs before they were required to do so by federal law. Massachusetts became the first state to mandate (命令) bilingual education in 1971. The ways in which bilingual programs are implemented by the different states varies greatly.

One of the most common models of bilingual education in the United States is called transitional bilingual education. In this kind of program, students learn ESL while taking all their other classes in their native language. Students must stop taking classes in their native language after some period of time, usually three years. After the three-year time limits, students start taking all their classes in English only. The reasoning for this model is that native language classes should serve only as a transition to English. The main goal of a transitional program is to teach students English as quickly as possible.

Another kind of program is called maintenance bilingual education. Maintenance programs do not have the same time limits as transitional programs. Students can continue taking content-area classes (science, mathematics, and social studies) in their native language for as long as they need to or want to. The idea behind a maintenance program is that a children native language is worth maintaining and developing. In fact, research has shown that students who are fully literate in their first language will be more successful in learning how to read and write with a second language. One of the problems with maintenance programs is that they are more expensive than transitional programs.

Two-way bilingual education is a program which offers second language instruction to students whose native language is English, while at the same time providing ESL to students who speak a language other than English. For example, English-speaking students take ESL classes. Both groups would continue to take their other content courses in their native language. In some classes, students may work together using both languages. The purpose of two-way bilingual educational programs is to make all students bilingual.

Finally, there is immersion bilingual education. In these programs, students take all-English courses for a year or two before they begin taking courses in their native language. In other words, they are immersed in English for the first year or two. Research has not shown that this kind of approach is more effective than the other models already described. Many students feel

大学英语 快速阅读 教程（4）

overwhelmed during the first two years. While struggling to learn English, they lose valuable time that should be spent learning important concepts in math and science.

Bilingual education has always been and continues to be a controversial (有争议的) subject. It is controversial for a variety of reasons. Some critics argue that bilingual education places an unfair burden on schools, and that taxpayers' money should not be spent teaching immigrants in their native language. They reason that all people in the United States should have to read, write, and speak English. In addition, they point out that bilingual programs haven't always been successful in producing literate, bilingual students.

Many people in favor of bilingual education agree that some bilingual programs are better than others, and not all of them are successful. However, research has proven that students who are literate in their first language will learn how to read and write a second language more easily. In addition, students who learn important concepts in math and science in their native language will be able to understand these concepts much more easily when they move into all-English courses. Some proponents (支持者) of bilingual education argue that the real reason critics are opposed to these programs is that these programs really work. Bilingual proponents say that critics of bilingual education do not really want immigrants to be successful at school.

The controversy over bilingual education continues. In 1998, a law was passed in California that made bilingual education illegal. According to this law, teachers are not allowed to teach students in any language other than English. Instead, students who speak a language other than English are allowed to take one year of ESL. After that, they must take all their courses in regular English.   (800 words)

Exercises

For questions 1-5, read the following statements, mark Y (for YES) if the statement agrees with the information given in the passage; N (for NO) if the statement contradicts the information given in the passage; NG (for NOT GIVEN) if the information is not given in the passage.

_____ 1. Two-way bilingual education enables all students to learn a foreign language including English-speaking students.

_____ 2. Immersion bilingual education is more successful than other models because students' skills in English are excellent since students have to learn English for the first year or two.

_____ 3. Research has proven that students can learn English more quickly and better if they learn it intensively while putting their native language aside.

_____ 4. Under the 1998 California law, students speaking a language other than English can take classes in their native language for one year.

_____ 5. Because of the huge influx of immigrants, different types of bilingual education come into being to suit different levels of English.

▶ *For questions 6-10, complete the sentences with the information given in the passage.*

6. Bilingual education refers to _____.

7. In the transitional bilingual education program, students usually can take classes in their native language for _____ years, and after that, they must _____.

8. Maintenance bilingual education differs from transitional bilingual education in that _____.

9. Opponents to bilingual education believe that all people in the United States should have to _____.

10. The problem with immersion bilingual education is _____.

Unit Five

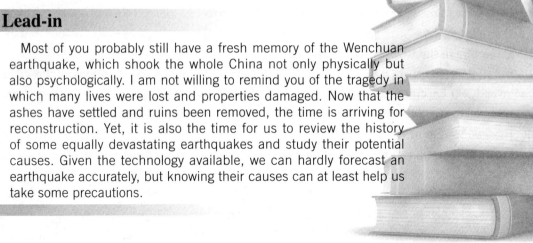

Lead-in

Most of you probably still have a fresh memory of the Wenchuan earthquake, which shook the whole China not only physically but also psychologically. I am not willing to remind you of the tragedy in which many lives were lost and properties damaged. Now that the ashes have settled and ruins been removed, the time is arriving for reconstruction. Yet, it is also the time for us to review the history of some equally devastating earthquakes and study their potential causes. Given the technology available, we can hardly forecast an earthquake accurately, but knowing their causes can at least help us take some precautions.

Section A

Passage One

Tectonics of the Wenchuan Earthquake

The extent of the Wenchuan earthquake and after-shock-affected areas lies north-east, along the Longmen Shan fault (地壳中的断层).

According to China Earthquake Administration:

The energy source of the Wenchuan earthquake and Longmen Shan's southeast push came from the strike of the Indian Plate onto the Eurasian Plate and its northward push. The inter-plate relative motion caused large scale structural deformation inside the Asian continent, resulting in a thinning crust (地壳) of the Qinghai-Tibet Plateau, the uplift of its landscape and an eastward extrude (挤压成形). Near the Sichuan Basin, Qinghai-Tibet Plateau's east-northward movement meets with strong resistance from the South China Block, causing a high degree of stress accumulation in the Longmen Shan thrust formation. This finally caused a sudden dislocation in the Yingxiu-Beichuan fracture, leading to the violent earthquake of 8.0 on the Richter scale.

According to the United States Geological Survey:

The earthquake occurred as the result of motion on a northeast striking reverse fault or thrust fault on the northwestern margin of the Sichuan Basin. The earthquake's epicenter (震中) and focal-mechanism are consistent with it having occurred as the result of movement on the Longmen Shan fault or a tectonically related fault. The earthquake reflects tectonic (构造) stresses resulting from the convergence of crustal material slowly moving from the high Tibetan Plateau, to the west, against strong crust underlying the Sichuan Basin and southeastern China. On a continental scale, the seismicity (地震活动) of central and eastern Asia is a result of northward convergence of the Indian Plate against the Eurasian Plate with a velocity of about 48 mm/year. The northwestern margin of the Sichuan Basin has previously experienced destructive earthquakes. The magnitude (震级) 7.6 earthquake of August 25, 1933 killed more than 9,300 people.

According to the British Geological Survey:

The earthquake occurred 92 km northwest of the city of Chengdu in eastern Sichuan Province and over 1,500 km from Beijing, where it was also strongly felt. Earthquakes of this size have the potential to cause extensive damage and loss of life. The epicenter was in the mountains of the Eastern Margin of Qing-Tibet Plateau at the northwest margin of the Sichuan Basin. The earthquake occurred as a result of motion on a northeast striking thrust fault that runs along the margin of the basin. The seismicity of central and eastern Asia is caused by the northward movement of the India plate at a rate of 5 cm/year and its collision with Eurasia, resulting in the uplift of the Himalaya and Tibetan plateau and associated earthquake activity. This deformation also results in the extrusion of crustal material from the high Tibetan Plateau in the west towards the Sichuan Basin and southeastern China. China frequently suffers large and deadly earthquakes. In August 1933, the magnitude 7.5 Diexi earthquake, about 90 km northeast of today's earthquake, destroyed the town of Diexi and surrounding villages, and caused many landslides, some of which dammed the rivers.   (512 words)

Exercises

For questions 1-7, read the following statements, mark Y (for YES) if the statement agrees with the information given in the passage; N (for NO) if the statement contradicts the information given in the passage; NG (for NOT GIVEN) if the information is not given in the passage.

_____ 1. It is a consensus among the three agencies that the earthquake was caused by the Indian Plate striking onto the Eurasian Plate.

_____ 2. According to the text, as a result of the Indian Plate striking onto the Eurasian Plate, the Qinghai-Tibet Plateau moves eastward, and meets strong resistance from the South China Block.

_____ 3. According to the text, the direct cause of the earthquake is a sudden dislocation in the Yingxiu-Beichuan fracture.

_____ 4. All the three agencies mentioned the uplift of the Qinghai-Tibet Plateau in their analysis.

_____ 5. Both the British Geological Survey and the United States Geological Survey determined the velocity of the northward movement of the India Plate is at a rate of 5 cm/year.

_____ 6. The velocity of northward convergence of the Indian Plate against the Eurasian Plate will be stable, even, and not likely to see a sudden acceleration.

_____ 7. As to the magnitude of the earthquake that took place on August 25, 1933, the United States Geological Survey differed with the British Geological Survey.

大学英语 快速阅读 教程（4）

▶ *For questions 8-10, there are three definitions below each underlined word in the passage. One definition is closest to its meaning. One definition has the opposite or nearly opposite meaning. The remaining definition has a completely different meaning. Label the definitions C for closest, O for opposite, and D for different.*

8. The inter-plate relative motion caused large scale structural deformation inside the Asian continent, resulting in a thinning crust of the Qinghai-Tibet Plateau, the uplift of its landscape and an eastward extrude.

_____ A) Plato

_____ B) tableland

_____ C) lowland

9. The earthquake reflects tectonic stresses resulting from the convergence of crustal material slowly moving from the high Tibetan Plateau, to the west, against strong crust underlying the Sichuan Basin and southeastern China.

_____ A) gathering

_____ B) departure

_____ C) convolution

10. The earthquake occurred as a result of motion on a northeast striking thrust fault that runs along the margin of the basin.

_____ A) edge

_____ B) march

_____ C) center

Passage Two

The Earthquake-damaged Panda Reserve Plans a Move

The world's most famous panda reserve wants to find a new home after its current one was badly damaged by this month's deadly earthquake in China.

"It's better to move, I think," Zhang Hemin, the chief of the Wolong Reserve, said by phone on Thursday.

A state-run news agency also reported on Thursday that another panda reserve, China's largest, has had to call off patrols and its annual panda census (统计) because of the quake's aftershocks.

The Wolong Reserve is just 20 miles from the epicenter of the May 12 quake, which has killed more than 68,000 people, including five reserve staff members.

One panda remains missing. Conditions remain so bad that the Chinese government last week arranged an emergency food shipment of about 5 tons of bamboo for the 47 pandas still at the reserve. Many panda enclosures were heavily damaged.

"What I'm worrying about are secondary disasters, such as severe aftershocks," Zhang said. "The road is easily blocked by rocks falling from the mountain. There would be no way to get the food in."

The reserve's location in a damp, narrow valley several hours' drive from the capital of Sichuan Province made it an easy target during the 7.9-magnitude quake, which tossed down boulders (巨石) the size of cars. Most of the staffers, tourists and pandas were outside at the time.

According to an article by the only journalist at the reserve during the quake, *Shanghai Morning Post*'s Wu Fei, some pandas froze and looked at the sky, not moving even when their handlers (训练员) tried to get them going.

Other handlers picked up baby pandas by the scruff (颈背) of their necks, one in each hand, and ran, Wu said in his article published on May 18.

"The on-the-spot rescue was complicated because some of the pandas were in what the Chinese call their 'falling in love period', being particularly excitable and prone to attack," the reserve researcher Heng Yi told Wu for the article.

After the earthquake, some pandas have been moved to another breeding center in Chengdu, and eight were flown to Beijing for a previously scheduled six-month stay at the Beijing Zoo for the Olympics.

"Meanwhile, any move of the Wolong Reserve has to wait for a damage assessment by geologists," Zhang said.

Another panda reserve, China's largest, has been forced to cancel its patrols and annual panda census because of aftershocks and blocked roads, the state-run Xinhua News Agency reported.

"We've not been able to get into the heart of the forests to check if the giant pandas are OK," Huang Huali, deputy director of the Baishuijiang Nature Reserve Administration, told Xinhua.

The reserve is in Sichuan and neighboring Gansu Province and is about 62 miles from the quake's epicenter.

The rare panda is a powerful symbol of China. About 1,590 pandas are living in the wild, mostly in Sichuan and the western Province of Shaanxi. An additional 180 have been bred in captivity in hopes of increasing the species' chances of survival.   (513 words)

Exercises

For questions 1-5, read the following statements, mark Y (for YES) if the statement agrees with the information given in the passage; N (for NO) if the statement contradicts the information given in the passage, NG (for NOT GIVEN) if the information is not given in the passage.

_____ 1. Struck by the earthquake, the pandas in the Wolong Reserve panicked, running riot.

_____ 2. No one was hurt since most of the staffers, tourists and pandas were outside when the earthquake occurred.

_____ 3. The earthquake has done irrevocable damages to the panda reserve and the species.

_____ 4. Wolong Reserve is the largest reserve of this type.

_____ 5. According to the text, the total number of pandas approximates to 1770.

▶ *For questions 6-10, complete the sentences with the information given in the passage.*

6. It had been difficult to get in the emergency food because _____.

7. The rescue of the pandas was a little difficult because some pandas that were in the "falling in love period" were _____ and _____.

8. The Wolong Reserve hasn't decided on any movement because it has to _____.

9. The Baishuijiang Nature Reserve has been forced to cancel its patrols and annual panda census because of _____ and _____.

10. The Wolong Reserve is located in _____; the Baishuijiang Nature Reserve is located in _____, and they are _____ miles and _____ miles from the quake's epicenter respectively.

Section B

Passage One

What Causes Earthquakes?

An earthquake is the shaking of the ground caused by an abrupt shift of rock along a fracture in the Earth, called a fault. Within seconds, an earthquake releases stress that has slowly accumulated within the rock, sometimes over hundreds of years.

The size of an earthquake is indicated by a number called its magnitude. Magnitude is calculated from a measurement of either the amplitude or the duration (持续时间) of specific types of recorded seismic waves. Magnitude is determined from measurements made from seismograms and not on reports of shaking or interpretations of building damage. The intensity of an earthquake is a measure of the amount of ground shaking at a particular site, and it is determined from reports of human reaction to shaking, damage done to structures, and other effects.

The most widely-accepted theory of the causes of earthquake is the plate tectonics theory (板块构造学说).

The plate tectonics theory is a starting point for understanding the forces within the Earth that cause earthquakes. Plates are thick slabs (平板) of rock that make up the outermost 100 kilometers or so of the Earth. Geologists use the term "tectonics" to describe deformation of the Earth's crust, the forces producing such deformation, and the geologic and structural features that result.

Earthquakes occur only in the outer, brittle (脆的) portions of these plates, where temperatures in the rock are relatively low. Deep in the Earth's interior, convection (对流) of the rocks, caused by temperature variations in the Earth, induces stresses that result in movement of the overlying plates. The rates of plate movements range from about 2 to 12 centimeters per year and can now be measured by precise surveying techniques. The stresses from convection can also deform the brittle portions of overlying plates, thereby storing tremendous energy within the plates. If the accumulating stress exceeds the strength of the rocks comprising these brittle zones, the rocks can break suddenly, releasing the stored elastic energy as an earthquake.

Three major types of plate boundaries are recognized. These are called spreading, convergent, or transform, depending on whether the plates move away from, toward, or laterally past one another, respectively. Subduction occurs where one plate converges toward another plate, moves beneath it, and plunges as much as several hundred kilometers into the Earth's interior.

Ninety percent of the world's earthquakes occur along plate boundaries where the rocks are usually weaker and yield more readily to stress than do the rocks within a plate. The remaining 10 percent occur in areas away from present plate boundaries—like the great New Madrid, Missouri, earthquakes of 1811 and 1812, felt over at least 3.2 million square kilometers, which occurred in a region of southeast Missouri that continues to show seismic activity today.

The Cascadian subduction zone off the coast of Washington, Oregon, and northern California is a convergent boundary between the large North America plate and the small Juan de Fuca plate to the west. The Juan de Fuca plate moves northeastward and then plunges (subducts) obliquely beneath the North America plate at a rate of 3 to 4 centimeters per year.

Washington has features typical of convergent boundaries in other parts of the world.

It is established that there is a zone of deep earthquakes near the probably boundary between the Juan de Fuca plate and the North America plate. The 1949 magnitude 7.1 Olympic earthquake and the 1965 magnitude 6.5 Seattle-Tacoma earthquake occurred within this deep zone.

The active or recently active volcanoes of the Cascade range were caused by the upward migration of magma (molten rock) above the Juan de Fuca plate. Rock in the subducting plate may melt at depths of 100 kilometers or more in the Earth. Because melted rock is lighter, it can sometimes rise to the surface through weakened areas in the overlying materials.

Young, highly deformed mountains composed of formerly oceanic rocks scraped off the Juan de Fuca plate during subduction and piled up on the Olympic peninsula.

Deformed young sediments offshore in the Pacific Ocean where the converging plates meet.

In sum, the subduction of the Juan de Fuca plate beneath the North America plate is believed to directly or indirectly cause most of the earthquakes and young geologic features in Washington and Oregon.

(726 words)

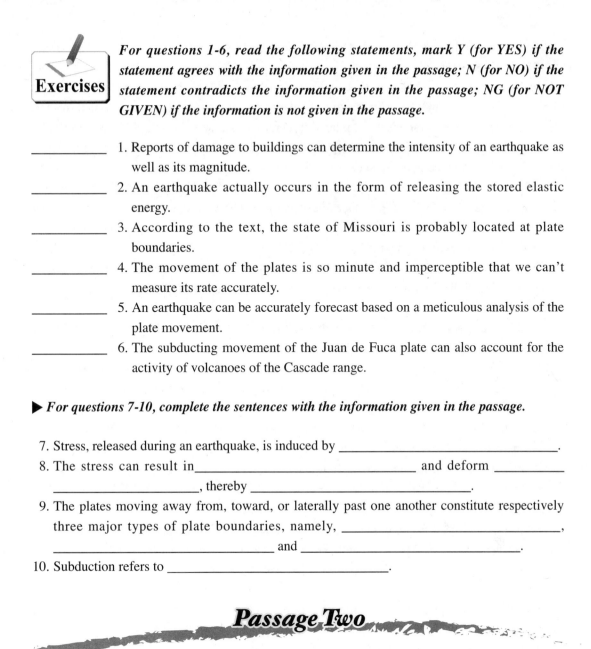

Unit Five

Exercises

For questions 1-6, read the following statements, mark Y (for YES) if the statement agrees with the information given in the passage; N (for NO) if the statement contradicts the information given in the passage; NG (for NOT GIVEN) if the information is not given in the passage.

_____ 1. Reports of damage to buildings can determine the intensity of an earthquake as well as its magnitude.

_____ 2. An earthquake actually occurs in the form of releasing the stored elastic energy.

_____ 3. According to the text, the state of Missouri is probably located at plate boundaries.

_____ 4. The movement of the plates is so minute and imperceptible that we can't measure its rate accurately.

_____ 5. An earthquake can be accurately forecast based on a meticulous analysis of the plate movement.

_____ 6. The subducting movement of the Juan de Fuca plate can also account for the activity of volcanoes of the Cascade range.

▶ *For questions 7-10, complete the sentences with the information given in the passage.*

7. Stress, released during an earthquake, is induced by _____.

8. The stress can result in_____ and deform _____ _____, thereby _____.

9. The plates moving away from, toward, or laterally past one another constitute respectively three major types of plate boundaries, namely, _____, _____ and _____.

10. Subduction refers to _____.

Passage Two

Famous Earthquakes in History

1556, Shaanxi Province, China

In the morning hours of February 14, 1556, a devastating earthquake rocked central China. Centered in Shaanxi Province, the earthquake affected some 500 miles and 10 provinces. The Shaanxi quake is estimated to have been magnitude 8.

To this day, the Shaanxi quake is known as the most devastating earthquake on record. It took 830,000 lives, destroyed entire communities. Most of its death toll may be attributed to living conditions in the region. Instead of living in villages, much of the populace lived in caves or under loose loess cliffs which collapsed as the quake shook the earth.

1755, Lisbon, Portugal

On November 1, 1755, Lisbon was nearly destroyed in total by an earthquake and the resulting tsunami and fire. The initial quake, estimated to have been magnitude 9, lasted for 3 to 6 minutes and was felt as far away as Finland. It literally tore Lisbon apart—giant fissures ripped across the city's center as the quake progressed. Cities across Portugal and southwestern Spain were also damaged in the initial quake.

In the aftermath of the quake, buildings in Lisbon collapsed and caught fire. The fires burned for five days, razing many old, irreplaceable structures. The violent seismic waves created an equally devastating tidal wave that hit the harbor areas of the city. 90,000 people were killed.

1906, San Francisco, California

The great San Francisco earthquake of 1906 is enshrined as a watershed disaster in American history. Striking in the early morning hours of April 18, the initial quake lasted nearly a minute. It was estimated to be a 7.9 magnitude quake.

Adding to the devastation was the fire that followed the earthquake. Many buildings in San Francisco were made of wood, were structurally unsound, and were either lit or warmed by wood, coal, and gas-burning devices. Upon collapsing, these buildings quickly went up in flames. The resulting conflagration burned for days after the quake, razing more than 4 square miles of the city before it was finally contained.

Modern estimates place the loss of life at over 500. In addition, the destruction resulted in looting incidents and other lawlessness throughout the city. To try and curb the crime during the weeks after the disaster, Mayor E. E. Schmitz actually issued a temporary "shoot to kill" order against anyone caught in the commission of a crime.

1960, Chile

Dubbed "the Largest Earthquake in the World", the Great Chilean Earthquake occurred just off the coast of Chile, on May 22, 1960. The quake's magnitude measured at 9.5, the highest ever recorded by seismologists. The quake was followed by seismic tidal waves that drowned the Chilean coast.

The destructive force of the quake reached all the way to Hawaii. In the end, more than 2,000 lives were lost to the Great Chilean Quake.

1964, Prince William Sound, Alaska

The largest earthquake in the United States history occurred off the coast of Alaska on March 27, 1964. The 9.2 magnitude quake, claiming 131 lives, lasted for 4 minutes, causing extensive damage to nearby Anchorage, and general damage to many of the towns and cities of Alaska. The quake also created seismic tidal waves that drowned the coast of Alaska.

The seismic tidal waves created by the Great Alaskan Quake caused extensive damage along the coast of British Columbia, Canada and the Pacific Northwestern United States.

2004, Indian Ocean

A recent major earthquake rumbled deep on the floor of the Indian Ocean on December 26, 2004. At an estimated magnitude of 9.3, it was the second strongest quake ever recorded by seismologists. Occurring more than 18 miles beneath the ocean, the quake itself was not particularly devastating.

While the quake itself may have caused some damage, the resulting seismic tidal wave it created was legendary. The Indian Ocean Tsunami struck dozens of countries, including parts of India, Indonesia, Thailand, and Sri Lanka. Waves measuring between 80 and 100 feet high struck the coastal areas. The force of the waves carried them more than a mile inland, in some areas. Thousands of communities were destroyed, or displaced; coastlines were completely reshaped by the force of the waters. Between 175,000 and 250,000 are believed to have perished, though a solid number may never be known, and no reliable estimate of damages yet exists.

Ultimately, the Indian Ocean Tsunami reached as far as South Africa to the west and Mexico to the east of the quake epicenter. Every ocean showed at least some measurable effect from the event. (747 words)

Exercises

For questions 1-10, choose the best answer from the four choices marked A), B), C) and D) according to the information given in the passage.

1. The casualties in the Shaanxi earthquake were extremely heavy because _____.
   A) riots broke out
   B) tidal waves took many lives
   C) a major conflagration broke out
   D) the living conditions in that region were special

2. Which is the largest earthquake in the United States?
   A) The San Francisco earthquake.   B) The Chilean earthquake.
   C) The Indian Ocean earthquake.   D) The Alaska earthquake.

3. Which of the following earthquakes claimed the largest number of lives?
   A) The San Francisco earthquake.   B) The Shaanxi earthquake.
   C) The Indian Ocean earthquake.   D) The Alaska earthquake.

4. Which of the following earthquakes caused the smallest casualties?
   A) The Lisbon earthquake.   B) The Shaanxi earthquake.
   C) The San Francisco earthquake.   D) The Indian Ocean earthquake.

5. Which of the following earthquakes didn't cause tidal waves?
   A) The San Francisco earthquake.   B) The Chilean earthquake.
   C) The Indian Ocean earthquake.   D) The Alaska earthquake.

6. The Indian Ocean earthquake is second in magnitude only to _____.
   A) the Shaanxi earthquake   B) the San Francisco earthquake
   C) the Chilean Earthquake   D) the Alaska earthquake

7. Which earthquake caused the most extensive damage?
   A) The Shaanxi earthquake.   B) The Indian Ocean earthquake.
   C) The Chilean earthquake.   D) The Alaska earthquake.

8. Which of the following earthquakes' magnitude was smallest?

    A) The San Francisco earthquake.   B) The Chilean earthquake.

    C) The Indian Ocean earthquake.   D) The Alaska earthquake.

9. Which of the following earthquakes did crimes ensue?

    A) The Shaanxi earthquake.   B) The San Francisco earthquake.

    C) The Chilean earthquake.   D) The Alaska earthquake.

10. Why was not the Indian Ocean earthquake itself particularly devastating?

    A) Because it took place far away from densely-populated area.

    B) Because the epicenter was located deep beneath the ocean.

    C) Because the earthquake occurred in the night.

    D) Because looting incidents caused more casualties than the quake.

Unit Six

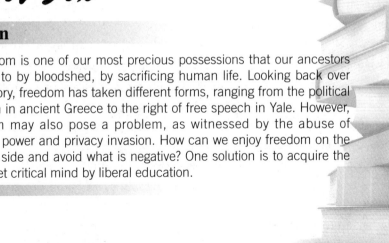

Lead-in

Freedom is one of our most precious possessions that our ancestors aspired to by bloodshed, by sacrificing human life. Looking back over the history, freedom has taken different forms, ranging from the political freedom in ancient Greece to the right of free speech in Yale. However, freedom may also pose a problem, as witnessed by the abuse of political power and privacy invasion. How can we enjoy freedom on the positive side and avoid what is negative? One solution is to acquire the broad yet critical mind by liberal education.

Section A

Passage One

Unbridled Free Speech Integral to Yale

I never thought I would say it, but today I am grateful for university president Richard Levin.

There are, perhaps, many reasons to be glad that we are at Yale now, rather than when Benno Schmidt was president. But a major one came on Monday, when *The New York Times* printed a letter from Schmidt, now vice-president of the City University of New York (CNUY) Board of Trustees (理事会), defending that body's decision to publicly denounce the CUNY faculty ([大学的]全体教师) who questioned the war in Afghanistan.

The CUNY board was responding to an article by *The New York Post* about a teach-in (大学师生举行的时事宣讲会) organized by the CUNY professors' union, the Professional Staff Congress. *The Post* reported that the faculty at the meeting attacked U.S. foreign policy and suggested that the past American policy helped precipitate the Sept. 11 terrorist attacks.

The chancellor (校长) and board of CUNY responded by saying that the professors "brought shame to the City University of New York".

Whether one agrees or disagrees with the professors' sentiments, it is a dangerous day when the governing body of a university attacks its faculty for speaking.

Thankfully, Yale's traditions of academic freedom do not allow such attacks.

For the most part, Yale has always been a strong defender of academic freedom. At the height of the Cold War, the master of Branford College was a committed Communist (共产党员). It is hard to imagine that happening at many other universities at a time when, even with the protections of tenure ([教师的]终身任职权), schools were encouraged to purge (肃清) leftists (左翼).

Indeed, we at Yale are blessed with dozens of opinions. Departments like history, religious studies, and the Medical School's Psychiatry (物理治疗学) have all sponsored panels. We have had master's teas featuring experts on diplomacy, terrorism, and the Taliban. We hear from the right and the left on this page.

Discussion and a search for truth is what a university is supposed to be about. Sometimes we agree, sometimes we argue, and at times, we can even become disgusted with each other's views. But the beauty of the university is that it is a safe heaven for people to question their society and their government.

It is contrary to the spirit of the university's underlying principles of free inquiry and academic liberty to reduce one's opponent's arguments to "hate speech".

For the same reason, the CUNY board and chancellor were wrong to attack the school's faculty for holding a teach-in and having the audacity (胆大妄为) to criticize their country's government.

Although Yale has a proud tradition of academic freedom, we must remain ever vigilant against encroachments (侵犯). Yale's record has not always been perfect, and will likely not remain so.

In the mid-1990s, graduate students who favored unionization were given negative recommendations in retaliation. A group of Yale radiologists (放射科医师) have filed suit saying, among other things, that they were silenced for raising concerns about procedures at the Medical School.

Beyond the Yale administration's history of sometimes silencing those with whom it disagrees, there is a broader danger in acquiescing (默认) to censorship (审查[制度]). A long tradition of anti-intellectualism in American society makes universities easy targets when things go wrong. The current "war on terrorism", like the Vietnam War before it and the McCarthyism[1] 1950s before that, threatens to be such a time.

It has been suggested that leftists and pacifists (反战主义者) in academia are out of step with the American people and so, it is argued, they should be quiet, conform, or perhaps even leave the country. That is the start of a dangerous trend.

The University must, in order to retain its integrity, refuse to merely go along with what others are saying. Academics have the obligation to question; scholars have the obligation to reject the American tradition of anti-intellectualism.

We must stand up to that tradition and every day reaffirm (重申) our right to question, to study, and to raise uncomfortable questions. If we allow ourselves to be silenced, if we fail to ask what others do not want to hear, we will let the terrorists win.

(767 words)

Note:

① McCarthyism（麦卡锡主义）是在 20 世纪 50 年代初，由美国参议员约瑟夫·麦卡锡（Joseph Raymond McCarthy）煽起的美国全国性反共"十字军运动"。他任职参议员期间，大肆渲染共产党侵入政府和舆论界，促使成立"非美调查委员会"（House Committee on Un-American Activities），在文艺界和政府部门煽动人们互相揭发，许多著名人士受到迫害和怀疑。

Exercises

For questions 1-6, there are three definitions below each underlined word in the passage. One definition is closest to its meaning. One definition has the opposite or nearly opposite meaning. The remaining definition has a completely different meaning. Label the definitions C for closest, O for opposite, and D for different.

1. Unbridled Free Speech <u>Integral</u> to Yale

_____ A) essential

_____ B) coherent

_____ C) dispensable

2. At the height of the Cold War, the master of Branford College was a <u>committed</u> Communist.

_____ A) vengeful

_____ B) devoted

_____ C) disloyal

3. Although Yale has a proud tradition of academic freedom, we must remain ever <u>vigilant</u> against encroachments.

_____ A) unwary

_____ B) vagrant

_____ C) watchful

4. In the mid-1990s, graduate students who favored unionization were given negative recommendations in <u>retaliation</u>.

_____ A) revenge

_____ B) repetition

_____ C) condone

5. It has been suggested that leftists and pacifists in academia are out of step with the American people and so, it is argued, they should be quiet, <u>conform</u>, or perhaps even leave the country.

_____ A) confront

_____ B) obey

_____ C) dissent

6. The University must, in order to <u>retain</u> its integrity, refuse to merely go along with what others are saying.

_____ A) keep on

_____ B) set in

_____ C) let go

▶ *For questions 7-10, read the following statements, mark Y (for YES) if the statement agrees with the information given in the passage; N (for NO) if the statement contradicts the information given in the passage; NG (for NOT GIVEN) if the information is not given in the passage.*

7. The author condemns the CUNY Board of Trustees, which denounced its faculty who questioned the war in Afghanistan, while praising Yale's academic freedom.

8. Having a committed Communist as the master of Branford College at the height of the Cold War reflected Yale's tradition of academic freedom.

9. Yale never deviated from its tradition of academic freedom throughout its history.

10. The author appeals to the universities and students to carry forward the tradition of academic freedom and every day reaffirms their right to question, to study, and to raise uncomfortable questions.

Passage Two

Wiretapping in the U.S. History

Wiretaps (搭线窃听) have had a long and complex history in U.S. jurisprudence (法学). Their first use was in the mid-19th century, in response to the invention of the telegraph. Shortly afterward, they appeared in war: Confederate General Jeb Stuart traveled with his own wiretapper to tap Union army lines. Wiretaps came into their own during Prohibition[①], the period between 1920 and 1933 in which the manufacture and sale of alcohol was illegal. Federal law-enforcement agents discovered the value of wiretaps in both investigating and prosecuting (起诉) bootlegging (走私漏税) cases. The Olmstead case set the stage for the next 40 years of U.S. wiretap law.

In the 1920s, Roy Olmstead had a major bootlegging operation in Seattle. Federal agents wiretapped Olmstead and his co-conspirators (同谋), placing taps in the basement of his office building and on telephone poles outside private houses. Olmstead's lawyers argued their case on the basis of the Fourth Amendment to the U.S. Constitution (美国宪法第四修正案) which goes:

The right of the people to be secure in their persons, houses, papers and effects against unreasonable searches and seizures (扣押) shall not be violated, and no warrants shall issue but upon probable cause, supported by oath (誓言) or affirmation, and particularly describing the place to be searched, and the persons or things to be seized.

The U.S. Supreme Court held that wiretaps were not a form of search, and thus didn't require search warrants. But the most well-known opinion in the Olmstead case isn't that of the majority, but of Justice Louis Brandeis' dissent. He said that wiretaps were a special type of search:

The evil incident to invasion of privacy of the telephone is far greater than that involved in tampering with the mails. Whenever a telephone line is tapped, the privacy of persons at both ends of the line is invaded, and all conversations between them upon any subject, and although proper, confidential, and privileged, may be overheard. Moreover, the tapping of one man's telephone line involves the tapping of the telephone of every other person whom he may know or who may call him. As a means of espionage, writs (法院的令状) of assistance and general warrants are but puny (微不足道的) instruments of tyranny and oppression (压制) when compared with wiretapping.

—Olmstead v. United States

A decade later, citing the 1934 U.S. Federal Communications Act (联邦通讯法), which prohibited the "interception (拦截) and divulgence (泄露)" of wired communications, the U.S. Supreme Court overturned the Olmstead decision in the Nardone cases[2]. In a series of cases over the next 30 years, the Supreme Court also slowly narrowed the circumstances under which law enforcement could perform electronic bugging without a warrant, until 1967, in *Charles Katz* v. *United States*[3] when the Court concluded that an electronic bug (窃听器) in even so public a place as a phone booth was indeed a search and therefore should be protected under the Fourth Amendment.

The Court's rulings of the 1930s did not end law enforcement wiretapping; instead, tapping went underground figuratively as well as literally. After the Nardone rulings, law enforcement didn't publicly divulge wiretapped information (or, it did, but not the fact that the information came from wiretaps). This legal never-never land (理想的地方) led to abuses by FBI director J. Edgar Hoover's agents, including the wiretapping (and bugging) of political dissidents, Congressional staffers, and U.S. Supreme Court Justices. The FBI's extensive records on political figures were well known, and this information, some of which was salacious (淫秽的), ensured that Congress conducted little oversight of the FBI. When, in reaction to the Katz decision, Congress decided to pass a wiretapping law, the national legislature (立法机关) was quite concerned about preventing Hoover-era abuses.

(689 words)

Note:

① 从 1920 年 1 月 17 日凌晨 0 时，美国宪法第 18 号修正案——禁酒法案（又称"伏尔斯泰得法案"）正式生效。根据这项法律规定，凡是制造、售卖乃至于运输酒精含量超过 0.5% 以上的饮料皆属违法。自己在家里喝酒不算犯法，但与朋友共饮或举行酒宴则属违法，最高可被罚款 1,000 美元及监禁半年。1933 年 2 月，美国国会通过第二十一条宪法修正案以取消禁酒之第八修正案。次年，随着犹他州作为第三十六个州签署此弛禁法案，美国的全国性禁酒寿终正寝。

② 1934 年，美国国会通过的《联邦通讯法》对窃听的态度发生了急剧变化。在 *Nardone* v. *U.S.* 案中，最高法院认为，该条适用于联邦法律执行官员，执法官员在法庭上就窃取的谈话的内容进行作证是一种为该法所禁止的泄露窃听内容的行为，因而，这种证据是不可采用的。但按最高法院的解释，如果窃取的信息不在政府部门以外使用，窃听并不是非法的。

③ 在 1967 年的 *Katz* v. *U.S.* 案中，最高法院推翻了 Olmstead 案中两点判决意见，认为第四

条修正案保护的是个人的隐私权，而不是财产权，窃听同搜查和扣押一样，也构成了对被告人隐私权的侵犯，因而应受宪法第四修正案的约束。

For questions 1-6, read the following statements, mark Y (for YES) if the statement agrees with the information given in the passage; N (for NO) if the statement contradicts the information given in the passage; NG (for NOT GIVEN) if the information is not given in the passage.

_____ 1. Bootlegging refers to the illegal use of the bugs on people's telephones.

_____ 2. The Fourth Amendment to the U.S. Constitution protects people's right against unreasonable searches and seizures.

_____ 3. The law enforcement stopped disclosing wiretapped information after the Nardone rulings.

_____ 4. All the persons involved in the wiretapping cases lost their lawsuits.

_____ 5. As far as the practice of wiretapping is concerned, the supervision of the Congress on FBI was comparatively slack.

_____ 6. The practice of wiretapping will be stopped by the Congress in the future.

▶ *For questions 7-10, complete the sentences with the information given in the passage.*

7. In the Olmstead case, the taps were placed _____.

8. The dissent of Louis Brandeis from the U.S. Supreme Court is mainly focused on _____.

9. In the 1930s, although the "interception and divulgence" of wired communications was prohibited, wiretapping _____.

10. In 1967, the Court ruled that wiretapping in a phone booth _____.

Section B

Passage One

Intellectual Diversity and the Indispensable Role of Liberal Education

In any education of quality, students encounter an abundance of intellectual diversity—new knowledge, different perspectives, competing ideas, and alternative claims of truth. This intellectual diversity is experienced by some students as exciting and challenging, while others are confused and overwhelmed by the complexity. Liberal education (通才教育，人文教育), the nation's signature educational tradition, helps students develop the skills of analysis and critical inquiry with particular emphasis on exploring and evaluating competing claims and different perspectives. With its emphasis on breadth of knowledge and sophisticated habits of mind, liberal education is the best and most powerful way to build students' capacities to form their own judgments about complex or controversial questions. It is believed that all students need and deserve this kind of education, regardless of their academic major or intended career.

Liberal education involves more than the mind. It also involves developing students' personal qualities, including a strong sense of responsibility to self and others. Liberally educated students are curious about new intellectual questions, open to alternative ways of viewing a situation or problem, disciplined to follow intellectual methods to conclusions, capable of accepting criticism from others, tolerant of ambiguity (难以理解的感情或想法), and respectful of others with different views. They understand and accept the imperative (要求) of academic honesty. Personal development is a very real part of intellectual development.

Beyond fostering intellectual and personal development, a liberal education also enables students to develop meaning and commitments in their lives. In college they can explore different ways to relate to others, imagine alternative futures, decide on their intended careers, and consider their larger life's work of contributing to the common good.

Building such intellectual and personal capacities is the right way to warn students of the inappropriateness and dangers of indoctrination (教导), help them see through the distortions (曲解) of propaganda, and enable them to assess judiciously (明智而审慎地) the persuasiveness of powerful emotional appeals. Emphasizing the quality of analysis helps students see why unwelcome views need to be heard rather than silenced. By thoughtfully engaging diverse perspectives, liberal education leads to greater personal freedom through greater competence. Ensuring that college students are liberally educated is essential both to a deliberative (审慎的) democracy and to an economy dependent on innovation.

There are several misconceptions about intellectual diversity and academic freedom, and we address some of them here.

In an educational community, freedom of speech, or the narrower concept of academic freedom, does not mean the freedom to say anything that one wants. For example, freedom of speech does not mean that one can say something that causes physical danger to others. In a learning context, one must both respect those who disagree with oneself and maintain an atmosphere of civility. Anything less creates a hostile environment that limits intellectual diversity and, therefore, the quality of learning.

Students do not have a right to remain free from encountering unwelcome or "inconvenient questions", in the words of Max Weber. Students who accept the literal truth of creation narratives do not have a right to avoid the study of the science of evolution in a biology course; anti-Semites (反犹太主义者) do not have a right to a history course based on the premise (前提) that the Holocaust ([二战时纳粹对犹太人的]大屠杀) did not happen. Students protesting their institution's sale of clothing made in sweatshops ([劳动条件差而工资低的]血汗工厂) do not have a right to interrupt the education of others. Students do have a right to hear and examine diverse opinions, but within the frameworks that knowledgeable scholars—themselves subject to rigorous standards of peer review—have determined to be reliable and accurate. That is, in considering what range of views should be introduced and considered, the academy is guided by the best knowledge available in the community of scholars.

All competing ideas on a subject do not deserve to be included in a course or program, or to be regarded as equally valid just because they have been asserted. For example, creationism (神造天地论), even in its modern guise (外表) as "intelligent design", has no standing among experts in the life sciences because its claims cannot be tested by scientific methods. However, creationism and intelligent design might well be studied in a wide range of other disciplinary (学科的) contexts such as the history of ideas or the sociology of religion.

While the diversity of topics introduced in a particular area of study should illustrate the existence of debate, it is not realistic to expect that undergraduate students will have the opportunity to study every dispute (争论) relevant to a course or program. The professional judgment of teachers determines the content of courses. (854 words)

Exercises

For questions 1-6, read the following statements, mark Y (for YES) if the statement agrees with the information given in the passage; N (for NO) if the statement contradicts the information given in the passage; NG (for NOT GIVEN) if the information is not given in the passage.

_____ 1. According to the text, liberal education refers to those subjects of humanities, such as philosophy and literature.

_____ 2. Intellectual freedom encourages freedom of speech; therefore vernal attack to your opponents is welcome in a debate.

_____ 3. According to the text, students should always pursue accurate and tested doctrines while rejecting inaccurate ones.

_____ 4. Different ideas can compete with one another and coexist in different disciplinary contexts.

_____ 5. It is up to the teachers to decide the content of courses since their judgment is more professional.

_____ 6. The text is about the importance of conducting academic discussions when differences arise.

▶ *For questions 7-10, there are three definitions below each underlined word or phrase in the passage. One definition is closest to its meaning. One definition has the opposite or nearly opposite meaning. The remaining definition has a completely different meaning. Label the definitions C for closest, O for opposite, and D for different.*

7. There are several misconceptions about intellectual <u>diversity</u> and academic freedom, and we address some of them here.

_____ A) oneness

_____ B) variety

_____ C) ambiguity

8. In a learning context, one must both respect those who disagree with oneself and maintain an atmosphere of <u>civility</u>.

    _____ A) facetiousness

    _____ B) rudeness

    _____ C) politeness

9. Students do have a right to hear and examine diverse opinions, but within the frameworks that <u>knowledgeable</u> scholars—themselves subject to rigorous standards of peer review—have determined to be reliable and accurate.

    _____ A) scholarly

    _____ B) ignorant

    _____ C) faithful

10. Students do have a right to hear and examine diverse opinions, but within the frameworks that knowledgeable scholars—themselves <u>subject to</u> rigorous standards of peer review—have determined to be reliable and accurate.

    _____ A) insusceptible to

    _____ B) exposed to

    _____ C) afraid of

Passage Two

Roots of Freedom

Greece Discovered Freedom

Some 2,500 years ago Greece discovered freedom. Before that there was no freedom. There were great civilizations, splendid empires, but no freedom anywhere. Egypt, Babylon, Nineveh①, were all tyrannies (暴权), one immensely powerful man ruling over the helpless masses. In Greece, in Athens, a little city in a little country, there were no helpless masses, and a time came when the Athenians were led by a great man who did not want to be powerful. Absolute obedience to the ruler was what the leaders of the empires insisted on. Athens said no, there must never be absolute obedience to a man except in war. There must be willing obedience to what is good for all.

How Freedom Was Possible in Greece?

Athenians willingly obeyed the written laws which they themselves passed, and the unwritten, which must be obeyed if free men live together. They must show each other kindness and pity and the many qualities without which life would be intolerable except to a hermit (隐士) in the desert. The Athenians never thought that a man was free if he could do what he wanted. A man was free if he was self-controlled. To make yourself obey what you approved was freedom. They were saved from looking at their lives as their own private affair. Each one felt responsible for the welfare of Athens, not because it was imposed on him from outside, but because the city was his pride and his safety. The creed (信念) of the first free government in the world was liberty for all men who could control themselves and would take responsibility for the state. This was the conception that underlay the lofty reach of Greek genius.

The Loss of Freedom

But discovering freedom is not like discovering atomic bombs. It cannot be discovered once for all. If people do not prize it, and work for it, it will depart. Eternal vigilance is its price. Athens changed. It was a change that took place unnoticed though it was of utmost importance, a spiritual change which penetrated the whole state. It had been the Athenians' pride and joy to give to their city. That they could get material benefits from her never entered their minds. There had to be a complete change of attitude before they could look at the city as an employer who paid her citizens for doing her work. Now instead of men giving to the state, the state was to give to them. What the people wanted was a government which would provide a comfortable life for them; and with this as the foremost object, ideas of freedom and self-reliance and responsibility were obscured to the point of disappearing. Athens was more and more looked on as a cooperative business possessed of great wealth in which all citizens had a right to share. If men insisted on being free from the burden of self-dependence and responsibility for the common good, they would cease (停止) to be free. Responsibility is the price every man must pay for freedom. It is to be had on no other terms. Athens, the Athens of Ancient Greece, refused responsibility; she reached the end of freedom and was never to have it again.

A Good Idea Would Remain

But, "the excellent becomes the permanent", Aristotle said. Athens lost freedom forever, but freedom was not lost forever for the world. A great American statesman, James Madison, in or near the year 1776 A.D. referred to "the capacity of mankind for self-government". No doubt he had not an idea that he was speaking Greek. Athens was not in the farthest background of his mind, but once a great and good idea has dawned upon man, it is never completely lost. Somehow, in this or that man's thought such an idea lives though unconsidered by the world of action. One can never be sure that it is not on the point of breaking out into action, only sure that it will do so sometime.

(578 words)

Note:

① Nineveh（尼尼微）是古亚述帝国的都城和文化中心，以巨大的建筑著称。亚述国王对在战争中不肯投降的战败国极其残酷，所以在犹太人和其他民族的书籍典故中，尼尼微被称为"血腥的狮穴"。

Exercises

For questions 1-7, read the following statements, mark Y (for YES) if the statement agrees with the information given in the passage; N (for NO) if the statement contradicts the information given in the passage; NG (for NOT GIVEN) if the information is not given in the passage.

_____ 1. The main purpose of this passage is to explain how freedom was discovered.

_____ 2. It was Greece that first discovered freedom.

_____ 3. In Greece, freedom was possible through enforcement of law and use of force.

_____ 4. Just like discovering atomic bombs, freedom can be discovered once and for all.

_____ 5. In looking at the city as an employer and a cooperative business, the Athenians lost freedom.

_____ 6. Material contribution is the price every man must pay for freedom.

_____ 7. Instead of taking responsibility for the state, the Athenians gradually began demanding material benefits from their country.

▶ *For questions 8-10, complete the sentences with the information given in the passage.*

8. _____ is the price of freedom.

9. If men insisted on being free from responsibility for the common good, they would _____.

10. Once a great and good idea has dawned upon man, it is _____.

Unit Seven

Lead-in

With the rapid advances in modern computer science and the Internet, many great changes have taken place in our daily life: We can watch TV online or bring the Internet to our television directly; we are informed of the Microsoft vs. Google competition and yet plagued by hacking now and then. Swirled around by the quick arrival of cutting-edge technologies, we must learn to adjust ourselves and keep pace.

Section A

Passage One

NBC's Web Tale

Burlingame, Calif.—Rosario Dawson, the hot actress from *Sin City* and *Death Proof*, panics. Her boyfriend is having some sort of seizure ([疾病的]突然发作) and she doesn't know what to do. But suddenly, the boyfriend flings forward and his hand closes around Dawson's neck. The transmission cuts out.

So ends the first five-minute episode of the science fiction-flavored *Gemini Division*, a new online TV show from NBC Universal①. The 50-episode series performs for the first time on Monday and is the first project to launch from NBC's four-month old digital studio.

The Network hopes *Gemini* will capture and expand upon the audiences drawn to Web shows like *Lonely Girl* and Michael Eisner's *Prom Queen*, while attracting the Network's creative talent and advertisers.

NBC, which also has a dozen other Web shows in the works, plans to scatter (撒播) *Gemini* across distribution channels, including NBC.com, SciFi.com, various Web portals and video-on-demand services like Microsoft marketplace on the Xbox 360. The show will rely on "brand integration"—product placement 2.0 (植入式广告), if you will—and other forms of advertising to underwrite (负担……的费用) the content.

Still, it's all one giant experiment for the Peacock Network. "No one knows the answer to this," says Cameron Death, vice president of NBC's digital studio. "We're all in this learning in real time and pushing the overall business forward."

Everyone, from amateurs to social networks like Bebo② to media giants such as Warner Bros.③ and CBS④, is dabbling (涉足) in short, episodic Web clips. "NBC is not the first mover and has the burden of ramping up (加速发生) the skill, but they have the benefit of seeing where others have failed and learning from that," says Jupiter Research analyst Bobby Tulsiani.

Death declined to provide production and advertising figures for its Web shows, but Tulsiani figures NBC likely isn't spending multimillions and that experimenting with online content is a sound strategic move.

Still, Death says NBC is being careful about product placements so as not to turn off viewers. The network is planning to weave brands throughout shows in such a way that they become integral parts of the story. NBC will do this in two ways: either inviting brands into the early stages of script writing or using brands as jumping-off points for building an entire series.

Death insists NBC is not sliding down a slippery slope toward "adver-programing". "I'm not going to put anything on any of the NBC platforms that I'm not proud to put the Peacock on," Death says.

"The gambit (策略), though, has the potential to turn traditional TV development on its head," says Tuna Amobi, a media analyst with Standard & Poor's Equity Research. Advertisers would become part of the development process, making them more apt to promote their products in and alongside Web content.

As a result, NBC will be watched closely. Amobi says, "The Web series needs to bring something extraordinary to the table, not only to justify how it will be monetized (使货币化), but also to address some of the concerns advertisers have." (545 words)

Note:

① NBC（National Broadcasting Company[美国] 全国广播公司），成立于 1926 年，是美国一家主流广播电视网络公司。NBC 于 2004 年与法国的维旺迪环球旗下的娱乐部门合并，变更为 NBC Universal（NBC 环球），向下属 200 多家美国电视台提供节目。但在一些节目中 NBC 仍会使用它 "全国广播公司" 的全称。NBC 以孔雀为标志，所以 the Peacock Network 常被用来代称 NBC Universal。

② www.bebow.com 目前是英国最大的社交网站之一，是爱尔兰和新西兰第一大社交网站，同时也是美国第三大社交网站。

③ Warner Bros. 华纳兄弟影业公司

④ CBS 是 Columbia Broadcasting System（美国哥伦比亚广播公司）的缩写。CBS 是美国三大商业广播电视公司之一，1927 年成立，总部设在纽约。

Exercises

For questions 1-6, read the following statements, mark Y (for YES) if the statement agrees with the information given in the passage; N (for NO) if the statement contradicts the information given in the passage; NG (for NOT GIVEN) if the information is not given in the passage.

_____ 1. NBC is going to spread *Gemini* through its own distribution channel—NBC. com.

_____ 2. Cameron Death, vice president of NBC's digital studio is planning to conduct the experiment in China.

_____ 3. The Network believes _Gemini_ will capture and expand upon the audiences drawn to Web shows like _Lonely Girl_ and Michael Eisner's _Prom Queen_, while attracting the Network's creative talent and advertisers.

_____ 4. By scattering _Gemini_ across distribution channels, NBC is learning in real time and pushing the overall business forward.

_____ 5. Advertisers would get involved in the development process, making them more apt to promote their products in and alongside Web content.

_____ 6. The Web series needs to justify how it will be monetized, and not to consider any of the concerns advertisers have.

▶ *For questions 7-10, there are three definitions below each underlined word in the passage. One definition is closest to its meaning. One definition has the opposite or nearly opposite meaning. The remaining definition has a completely different meaning. Label the definitions C for closest, O for opposite, and D for different.*

7. So ends the first five-minute <u>episode</u> of the science fiction-flavored _Gemini Division_, a new online TV show from NBC Universal.

_____ A) chapter

_____ B) series

_____ C) development

8. NBC, which also has a dozen other Web shows in the works, plans to scatter _Gemini_ across <u>distribution</u> channels, including NBC.com, SciFi.com, various Web portals and video-on-demand services like Microsoft marketplace on the Xbox 360.

_____ A) collecting

_____ B) broadcasting

_____ C) evolution

9. The show will rely on "brand <u>integration</u>"—product placement 2.0, if you will—and other forms of advertising to underwrite the content.

_____ A) combination

_____ B) collapse

_____ C) incorporation

10. Everyone, from <u>amateurs</u> to social networks like Bebo to media giants such as Warner Bros. and CBS, is dabbling in short, episodic Web clips.

_____ A) engineers

_____ B) professionals

_____ C) non-professionals

Intel, Yahoo! TV Dreams

SAN FRANCISCO—Intel and Yahoo! said on Wednesday they hope to solve the problem of how to bring the Internet to your television by serving up bite-sized snippets (简短的信息、新闻等)—dubbed widgets—rather than the whole Internet.

The plan, announced at the Intel Developer Forum here, pairs off the Web portal's (门户站点) widget service with fresh processors that the PC chip giant has crafted especially for televisions.

"The time is now to bring the Internet to television," declared Eric Kim, senior vice president and general manager of Intel's Digital Home Group.

Intel's new processor, called Intel Media Processor 3100, will be built around the same chip design used in most of the world's PCs and servers, and it will support high-definition video, high-end audio and 3-D graphics.

The plan is to lure away (诱惑) television manufacturers into a single chip that can do many of the things now handled by a grab bag (摸彩袋) of pricey (昂贵的) parts. The chip, formerly code-named Canmore, will cost $35 when bought in bulk, and Intel said it will start cranking out (制成) large numbers of the new chip in September.

Patrick Barry, Yahoo!'s vice president of connected TV, said the Web portal plans to take advantage of televisions built around Intel's new product to serve up a version of its Yahoo! widget service. The service is based on technology developed by Konfabulator, a start-up Yahoo! acquired in 2005 that serves up bite-sized slices of the Web. The service, however, is not the "wild, wild West of the PC Internet", Kim said.

While Kim said Intel can't talk yet about what its customers will do with the new chips, he said Sony, Samsung, Toshiba and Motorola are all "indicating they are committed to this platform". Kim said the chips will start appearing in televisions, set-top boxes and other television-connected gizmos (小发明) set to go on sale next year.

Intel and Yahoo! are hoping that pairing processors and widgets will crack the troublesome problem of how to get the interactivity and openness of the Internet on televisions. During a demo, the companies showed how users can push a button on a TV to view snippets of information from the Web and push another button for an up-close look.

Intel is also making a big push into movies—specifically, 3-D films. At the event on Wednesday, the chip maker talked up a new partnership with DreamWorks Animation (梦工厂动画公司) and said future animated movies from the studio would carry a new logo and brand—InTru™ 3D. The brand denotes new, more sophisticated computer animation made possible by Intel technology, Intel said. DreamWorks said last month it was switching its big animation operations to run on Intel chips. Previously it used technology supplied by Intel's rival Advanced Micro Devices (AMD).

Jeffrey Katzenberg, DreamWorks Animation's Chief Executive told an audience at the event that starting next year, all of DreamWorks' animated movies would be made in 3-D. He called the

大学英语 快速阅读 教程 (4)

new technology "the greatest innovation to occur in the movie business in 70 years". Katzenberg treated the audience to a brief 3-D clip of the upcoming DreamWorks film *Monsters vs. Aliens*, due out in March. Conference attendees watched the clip with special 3-D glasses they found under their seats.   (577 words)

Exercises

For questions 1-8, choose the best answer from the four choices marked A), B), C) and D) according to the information given in the passage.

1. Intel and Yahoo! said on Wednesday they hoped to solve the problem of how to bring the Internet to your_____.
   A) computer   B) television
   C) source   D) operating system

2. The plan pairs off the Web portal's widget service with _____ that the PC chip giant has crafted especially for televisions.
   A) fresh processors   B) hard disk
   C) source code   D) operating system

3. Intel's new processor, called Intel Media Processor 3100, will support _____.
   A) high-definition video   B) high-end audio
   C) 3-D graphics   D) A, B and C

4. Intel said it will start cranking out large numbers of the new chip in _____.
   A) November   B) October
   C) Autumn   D) September

5. DreamWorks Animation's Chief Executive _____ told an audience at the event that starting next year, all of DreamWorks' animated movies would be made in 3-D.
   A) Jeffrey Katzenberg   B) Bill Gates
   C) Patrick Barry   D) George Bush

6. Intel is also making a big push into _____.
   A) modern music   B) modern plays
   C) film editing   D) 3-D films

7. _____ is the greatest innovation to occur in the movie business in 70 years.
   A) InTru™ 3D   B) Yahoo's disk
   C) Sony's disk   D) Toshiba's disk

8. _____ watched the clip with special 3-D glasses they found under their seats.
   A) Some students   B) Some technologists
   C) Conference attendees   D) Scientists present

Section B

Passage One

Microsoft's Sneak Attack on Google

Forget about that $44 billion takeover bid for Yahoo. Microsoft's latest assault on Google is slier (狡诈的).

Since May Microsoft has been reimbursing (偿还) people up to half of the value of items they buy using its search technology. The trick isn't working. In July Google's share of all searches jumped to 60% from 53% a year ago, while Microsoft's share dropped to 12% from 13.6%, according to Nielsen Online.

Now comes Chief Executive Steve Ballmer's latest would-be Google-toppling (倒塌) tactics (after his failed bid to take over Yahoo): a sneak attack using the newly launched version of Microsoft's dominant (强大的，有优势的) Web browser, Internet Explorer. Ballmer is not portraying the updated browser as a Google destroyer, but many of its features turn out to be a crafty (狡猾的) way for people to get around using the most popular search service.

"We didn't design this with Google in mind," insists Internet Explorer Dean Hachamovitch. He adds, "It's not clear what the consequences might be."

The engineers in Redmond deserve a little more credit than Hachamovitch wants to give. The new browser comes with a search box in the upper right-hand corner and, just below that, a row of tiny signs for various search destinations, such as Yahoo, EBay and MySpace. You can select which destinations you want to include here.

If your search will likely end up in Wikipedia, for instance, with a single click over a little "W" you can search only that encyclopedia. Amazon.com displays items for sale. *The New York Times* shows parts of stories. So far, 27 Web sites have joined the drop-down column, including Facebook and Digg.

Microsoft is, uncharacteristically, keeping its hands off, giving Web sites the option to serve up results and customize how they appear. It also magnanimously (慷慨地) lets those sites take all the revenue from ads alongside the results. That is a sly stab at Google's business, though this kind of searching—where users already know where they want to go—doesn't yield especially lucrative (赚钱的) ads for Google.

Another Google-dodging feature in the new browser: Highlighting a street address on a Web page launches a map, with the default set (默认设置) to Microsoft's Live Maps (though you can change this default to Google Maps).

Internet Explorer is the most widely used browser. This gives Microsoft a nice advantage over Google. Just as Microsoft used its dominance in operating systems to get its browser onto millions of computers, it now can rely on that browser to offer Web software. Microsoft needs that weapon as Google invades its field with freebie (赠品，免费物) Web versions of word processors and spreadsheets.

Best do this while the dominance lasts. Firefox's market share jumped by a third in the last year to 19%, while Internet Explorer lost 6 percentage points to 73%. Still, even that rival gives it a little credit for the new browser. "They're playing catch-up (to try to match the performance of another competitor), but I'm glad they're playing," says John Lilly, chief executive of Mozilla, the publisher of Firefox. (548 words)

Exercises

For questions 1-8, complete the sentences with the information given in the passage.

1. In July Google's share of all searches jumped to 60% from 53% a year ago, while Microsoft's share dropped to _____ from 13.6%, according to Nielsen Online.
2. Microsoft uses _____ as a sneak attack against Google.
3. The new browser comes with _____ in the upper right-hand corner and, just below that, a row of tiny logos for various search destinations, such as Yahoo, EBay and MySpace.
4. So far, _____ Web sites have joined the drop-down column, including Facebook and Digg.
5. Microsoft is keeping its hands off, giving Web sites _____ to serve up results and customize how they appear.
6. _____ is the most widely used browser.
7. Just as Microsoft used its dominance in operating systems to get its browser onto millions of computers, it now can rely on _____ to offer Web software.
8. Firefox's market share jumped by _____ in the last year to 19%, while Internet Explorer lost 6 percentage points to 73%.

Passage Two

In Pictures: Hacking Without Technology

Hackers have a lot of fancy names for the technical exploits they use to gain access to a company's networks: cross-site scripting (跨站脚本), buffer overflows (缓存溢出) or the particularly evil-sounding SQL injection (SQL注入), to name a few. However, Johnny Long prefers a simpler entry point for data theft: the emergency exit door.

"By law, employees have to be able to leave a building without showing credentials (证件),"

Long says. "So the way out is often the easiest way in."

Cases of Hacking Without Technology

Case in point: Tasked with stealing data from an ultra-secure building armed with proximity card readers (感应读卡器), Long opted for an old-fashioned approach. Instead of looking for vulnerabilities (弱点) in the company's networks or trying to hack the card readers at the building's entrances, he and another hacker shimmied a wet washcloth on a hanger through a thin gap in one of its exits. Flopping the washcloth around, they triggered a touch-sensitive metal plate that opened the door and gave them free roam of the building. "We defeated millions of dollars of security with a piece of wire and a washcloth," Long recalls, joyfully.

In other instances, Long has joined employees on a smoke break, chatted with them casually, and then followed them into the building. Sometimes stealing data is as simple as wearing a convincing hard hat or walking onto a loading dock, before accessing an unsecured computer or photocopying a few sensitive documents and strolling out the front door.

Hacker and Protector As Well

Fortunately for his victims, the companies that Long invades are also his customers. As a penetration tester for Computer Sciences Corporation security team, Long is paid to probe weak points in a company's information security. His job as a "white-hat" hacker[①] is to think like the bad guys—the more evil genius he can summon up, the better.

Moreover, if tactics like tailing an employee through a backdoor or picking a lock with a washcloth don't seem like real hacking, Long would suggest fine-tuning the word's definition. To bring that other side of hacking to the public's attention, he wrote a manual also functioning as manifesto (声明，宣言) titled *No Tech Hacking*, which was published this week. The book's goal, aside from pumping Long's already significant notoriety (声名远扬) in the world of cyberpunks[②] and script kiddies[③], is to show that hacking isn't always the realm of high technology.

Instead, he argues, it's still rooted in old-fashioned observation and resourcefulness. To obtain a corporate password, for instance, a hacker can pose as an employee and call a company's help desk or simply look over an employee's shoulder while he's on his laptop at a local cafe. To access a network, Long will photograph an employee, fake his badge or even his uniform, and slip past the front door security to find an unguarded terminal.

"That kind of no-tech hacking isn't a new idea, but it's one worth remembering," says Jeff Moss, the organizer of cyber-security conferences Black Hat and Defcon[④]. "There's a tendency in our industry to focus on the latest and most interesting attack," he says. "But Johnny is trying to show that the simple security problems that were spotted a long time ago haven't gone away, and the bad guys will use whatever's available."

That's a lesson that the security industry should learn: The average cost of a data breach (数据失窃) rose to more than $6.3 million last year, up from $4.8 million in 2006, according to research by the Ponemon Institute. And physical security played a growing role: Lost or stolen equipment accounted for about half of those breaches last year.

With those kinds of costs at stake, hiring hackers like Long isn't cheap: For basic vulnerability assessment, CSC[⑤], which is based in El Segundo, California, charges a minimum of $35,000. For complete penetration testing, which often involves obtaining specific files to demonstrate a firm's security flaws, the team can charge as much as $90,000.

Why Do They Like the Job?

But for the most in-depth hacking missions against well-protected companies, Long and the rest of CSC's security team are also rewarded with the illicit (非法的) thrill of intrusion. "When you get that James Bond feeling of espionage (间谍行为), it's a huge adrenaline (肾上腺素) rush," he says. Long admits that the night before a major case, his team often watches the geek thriller sneakers (鬼鬼祟祟的人). "Penetration tests that involve a human element are so much more exciting than sitting in front of a computer screen, poking through a company's firewall."

As a kid in suburban Maryland during the 1980s, Long's hacking career began under less sensational circumstances. Surfing the pre-Web Internet, he browsed bulletin boards looking for pirated (非法复制的) copies of video games. To pay for the growing long distance bills from his modem, he started charging his Web surfing to calling card numbers that he found on semi-legal sites. And when those phone-card sites started forcing users to pay for access, he found ways to circumvent (规避，绕过) the sites' security measures.

Soon, the challenge of bypassing firewalls and accessing distant networks was more interesting than any video game. "I would be on my Commodore 64[⑤], talking to a Unix system somewhere far away," Long says. "It was like travelling—the fascination of being in a place with a different culture and speaking a different language."

Long's Personal Resume

When he graduated from high school, Long skipped college and got a job at a local university as a systems administrator. Before he was 20, he moved on to a major health insurance provider that was in the midst of bringing its systems onto the Internet. Long wrote up a report detailing all the company's security vulnerabilities. It was ignored by his superiors. Feeling demoralized (泄气的), he eventually left the company and landed at CSC's offices in Falls Church, Virginia.

At CSC, Long found his niche (适合的位置). In 1998, for instance, he suggested a simple social engineering method to gain access to a company's server that wasn't attached to the Internet. Long tracked down the name of the company's technical contact person on the Web, and made a phone call to its help desk pretending to be that person. The help desk's staff switched on the server's modem, and CSC's team was inside. "Once I connected with the security team, I brought some of the perspective that the security community was just starting to get then, a street-level hacker mentality (智力)," Long says.

From there, CSC began to experiment with the physical security hacks it now uses today, and Long began developing a set of techniques he calls "Google Hacking": using simple search engine queries to find hackable vulnerabilities in Web sites. Today CSC has one of the security industry's better-known penetration testing teams, and Long is a celebrity (名人) in hacker circles.

Simple Methods in Hacking

Since he first became a professional penetration tester, cyber-security has evolved dramatically, Long says. *No Tech Hacking* is partly about the latest social engineering methods used by a new generation of cyber-criminals. Instead of searching for holes in companies' increasingly tight security perimeters (防御带), their attacks are about drawing the target out, bringing employees to a compromised (泄露秘密) Web site that infects their network, or convincing an administrator to give away his or her password in an e-mail.

But the other lesson of the book, Long says, is that some things haven't changed. "No matter how savvy (精明的) we think we are, the oldest attacks are still possible, and they're still prevalent," he says. "The smartest systems are still falling for simple tricks, and that's what keeps us in business." (1369 words)

Note:

① 黑客界历来就有白帽子（white-hat）和黑帽子（black-hat）之说。所谓白帽子，就是了解黑客技术的安全专家，他们同样以黑客的身份出现，但并不进行攻击；而所谓黑帽子就是传统意义上的黑客，即网络攻击者。

② cyberpunk 一词由表示控制论（cybernetics）的 cyber 与表示摇滚乐流派的 punk 组合而成，译为"电脑朋克"或"赛伯朋克"。最初指将未来描绘成一个由计算机主宰一切的可怕社会的计算机科幻小说，现在也常用来指对权威和社会不满的计算机高手。

③ script kiddies 指利用其他黑客编写的程序对网络系统进行攻击的人，他们只知道使用这些程序，但看不懂它们。在很多黑客的观点中，他们不是黑客，所以黑客给他们起了个名字叫脚本小子。

④ 从 1992 年开始，世界黑客大会每年七、八月份都在美国拉斯韦加斯举行，参会的黑客与计算机安全专家达到五六千人，其中甚至包括美国国家安全局、国防部、联邦调查局在内的谍报、军事和公共安全机构的代表。大会的主要内容是黑客们相互交流攻破各种安全保护系统的心得，几十场的大大小小的讲座，以及黑客之间的安全攻防战。

⑤ Computer Science Center (CSC)（美国）计算机科学公司。

⑥ Commodore 64 是 Commodore 公司于 1982 年 1 月推出的一款家用电脑，里面曾出现过为数众多的经典电脑游戏。

Exercises

For questions 1-6, read the following statements, mark Y (for YES) if the statement agrees with the information given in the passage; N (for NO) if the statement contradicts the information given in the passage; NG (for NOT GIVEN) if the information is not given in the passage.

_____ 1. Data theft is always committed through hi-tech.

_____ 2. Long is so smart that he can steal data without having to search for vulnerabilities in the company's networks or trying to hack the card readers at the building's entrances.

_____ 3. Stealing data is as simple as wearing a convincing hard hat or walking onto a loading dock.

_____ 4. This kind of no-tech hacking is a practical new method.

_____ 5. According to Long, penetration tests that involve a human element are not so exciting as sitting in front of a computer screen, poking through a company's firewall.

_____ 6. Long started his career as soon as he graduated from university.

▶ *For questions 7-10, complete the sentences with the information given in the passage.*

7. Johnny Long prefers a simpler entry point for data theft: _____
   .

8. Long and another hacker defeated millions of dollars of security with _____
   _____.

9. To bring that other side of hacking to the public's attention, he wrote a manual also
   functioning as manifesto titled _____.

10. The smartest systems are still falling for _____ according
    to Long.

Unit Eight

Lead-in

With the financial storm raging the world, a fierce debate arose over the bailout effort, led by the $700B stimulus plan approved by the Bush government, to rescue the financial market. Beyond severely affecting the western world, the storm has also cast a shadow on China, the powerhouse of world economy over the past decade. As a matter of fact, the biggest emerging country is undergoing a downturn. Will the slowdown of Chinese economy help ease the inflationary pressure or add insult to the economic wound of global economy? Read the following passages, and you may find the answer.

 **Section A**

Passage One

U.S. Senators to Vote on Bailout

The U.S. Senate will vote on Wednesday on a version of a financial rescue package after the House of Representatives rejected the $700B plan.

The Senate version is expected to be similar to the House's initial plan, but will include some new measures to ease its passage through Congress.

One of those new clauses will raise the government's guarantee on savings from $100,000 to $250,000.

The vote comes after senior Democrats pledged to find a bipartisan (获得两党支持的) solution.

"Working together, we are confident we will pass a responsible bill in the very near future," Senator Harry Reid and House of Representatives Speaker Nancy Pelosi wrote to President George W. Bush.

The Senate is attaching the new plan to a bill that deals with renewable energy tax incentives (刺激).

If it passes, the House of Representatives could be under pressure to accept some of the changes when it meets on Thursday.

"However, some members of Congress are continuing to press for more fundamental changes, for instance for a system of insurance for bad loans, rather than the removal of the loans from the books of financial companies," says the BBC's Americas editor Justin Webb.

Earlier President Bush had warned of "painful and lasting" consequences for the U.S. should

Congress fail to agree a rescue plan.

The Dow Jones index closed up 4.7% on Tuesday, recouping some losses from Monday's rout, after the markets reacted favorably to the president's statement.

Markets in Japan and Australia saw gains as they opened on Wednesday morning, with the Nikkei (日经指数) climbing 1.2%.

Possible Momentum

Analysts say the Senate is more likely to pass the bill because senators are not facing the same pressure from voters as members of the House.

All representatives face re-election in November compared with only one-third of senators.

The measure will require 60 of the 100 senators to vote in favor in order to pass.

The BBC's Jonathan Beale, in Washington, says a positive vote in the Senate is likely to give the bill momentum when it goes back to the House.

Presidential candidates John McCain and Barack Obama, who both support Mr. Bush's efforts to bail out the economy, say they will return from campaigning to vote in the Senate.

"Not the End"

Mr. Bush said at the White House, "We are in an urgent situation and the consequences will grow worse each day if we do not act."

The economy was depending on "decisive action on the part of our government", he added.

He said he wanted to "assure our citizens and citizens around the world that this is not the end of the legislative process".

"Our country is not facing a choice between government action and the smooth functioning of the free market," he said.

"We're facing a choice between action and the real prospect of economic hardship for millions of Americans," he warned.

(492 words)

Exercises

For questions 1-6, read the following statements, mark Y (for YES) if the statement agrees with the information given in the passage; N (for NO) if the statement contradicts the information given in the passage; NG (for NOT GIVEN) if the information is not given in the passage.

_____ 1. The House of Representatives approved the $700B economic rescue plan though the Senate had rejected it.

_____ 2. The Senate version is expected to be similar to the House's initial plan, only adding some new measures to facilitate its passage through Congress.

_____ 3. The vote comes before senior Democrats pledged to find a bipartisan solution.

_____ 4. Senator Harry Reid and House of Representatives Speaker Nancy Pelosi were pessimistic about the pass of the bill.

_____ 5. If it passes, the House of Representatives could be under pressure to accept some of the changes.

_____ 6. President Bush explained why Congress would fail to agree a rescue plan.

▶ *For questions 7-10, there are three definitions below each underlined word in the passage. One definition is closest to its meaning. One definition has the opposite or nearly opposite meaning. The remaining definition has a completely different meaning. Label the definitions C for closest, O for opposite, and D for different.*

7. The U.S. Senate will vote on Wednesday on a <u>version</u> of a financial rescue package after the House of Representatives rejected the $700B plan.

_____ A) introduction

_____ B) edition

_____ C) original

8. The vote comes after senior Democrats <u>pledged</u> to find a bipartisan solution.

_____ A) refused

_____ B) deteriorated

_____ C) promised

9. The Dow Jones index closed up 4.7% on Tuesday, <u>recouping</u> some losses from Monday's rout, after the markets reacted favorably to the president's statement.

_____ A) compensating

_____ B) cooperating

_____ C) irredeemable

10. "We're facing a choice between action and the real <u>prospect</u> of economic hardship for millions of Americans," he warned.

_____ A) entertainment

_____ B) present situation

_____ C) future

Passage Two

Bailout Bust May Have a Benefit

Don't panic. By throwing out a deeply flawed bailout plan, the House may have created an opportunity to craft a more effective response to the financial crisis.

With credit markets frozen and the Dow Jones Industrials Index plummeting 777.68 points on Monday, the 228-205 defeat[①] of the rescue package appears to come at the worst possible time. Plenty of experts think the "no" vote has the power to wipe what little confidence remains in the markets.

But it also could lead policy makers, particularly Treasury Secretary (财政部长) Henry Paulson, to draw up a plan that more directly addresses the factors causing the financial system to fall apart.

After all, the bill voted down on Monday was unlikely to be a big help to the banking system.

81

The market, upon seeing its details, may already have come to that conclusion, since stocks were down on Monday before the House defeat.

If a better-thought-out plan emerges in the coming days, stocks' prices may touch bottom.

First, the Treasury has to recognize that it miscalculated and show that it is open to new ideas. The $700 billion package was meant to calm markets. But, for that to happen, the plan needed to be built and sold in a way that smoothed its passage through Congress.

Instead, the Treasury's first document incited opposition because it gave the department extraordinary powers. And it demanded almost no quid pro quo (交换条件) from participating banks.

Next, Congressional leaders who crafted the compromises to the Treasury's proposal now need to demand real concessions. The provisions limiting executive pay need to be stronger. And the bill needs to contain hard-and-fast arrangements for the government to be properly compensated, with equity stakes, for taking on toxic assets (不良资产).

This could damp (抑制) much of the popular outcry.

More important, Treasury needs to address the two big problems crippling the banking system: lack of liquidity (流动资金) and capital.

The market is even turning against large regional banks that seem able to make it through the crisis. In addition to having the Federal Reserve[2] lend liberally to them, the government needs to stanch (止住[液体]流出) deposit outflows, perhaps by temporarily guaranteeing all deposits.

That approach carries large risks, but it would buy the government time to push for consolidation in the banking system, something it has started with J.P. Morgan Chase's[3] purchase of Washington Mutual's[4] banking operations and Citigroup's[5] acquisition (获得) of Wachovia[6].

And, in a redrafted bill, the Treasury should demand that banks passing bad assets to the government simultaneously issue new equity (普通股) to bolster (强化) capital. Some banks won't be able to sell at any price, but many will find buyers if the government is backstopping their liquidity (流动性保底) and taking their worst assets.

(498 words)

Note:

① 2008 年 9 月 29 日，美国政府提出的 7,000 亿美元救市方案，在美国国会众议院的投票中以 228 票反对、205 票赞成被否决。这个自 1929—1933 年大萧条以来规模最大的政府干预行动受挫，加剧了金融市场上的恐慌情绪，导致股票市场遭受重挫。

② The Federal Reserve（美联储），是 the Board of Governors of The Federal Reserve System（联邦储备系统管理委员会）的简称。它是一个美国联邦政府机构，办公地点位于华盛顿特区。

③ J.P. Morgan Chase（摩根大通）是全球历史最长、规模最大的金融服务集团之一，由大通银行、J.P. 摩根公司及富林明集团在 2000 年合并组成。

④ Washington Mutual（华盛顿互助银行）建立于 1889 年，是美国最大的存、贷款机构。该银行由于股价大跌 87% 而严重亏损，于 2008 年倒闭。2008 年 9 月，被摩根大通收购。

⑤ Citigroup（花旗集团）是当今世界资产规模最大、利润最多、全球连锁性最高、业务门类最齐全的金融服务集团。它由花旗公司与旅行者集团于 1998 年合并而成。

⑥ Wachovia（瓦乔维亚银行）曾是美国第四大银行，2008 年底与 Wells Fargo（富国银行）合并。

Exercises

For questions 1-5, there are three definitions below each underlined word in the passage. One definition is closest to its meaning. One definition has the opposite or nearly opposite meaning. The remaining definition has a completely different meaning. Label the definitions C for closest, O for opposite, and D for different.

1. By throwing out a deeply flawed <u>bailout</u> plan, the House may have created an opportunity to craft a more effective response to the financial crisis.

_____ A) financial aid

_____ B) medical treat

_____ C) abandon

2. With credit markets frozen and the Dow Jones Industrials Index <u>plummeting</u> 777.68 points on Monday, the 228-205 defeat of the rescue package appears to come at the worst possible time.

_____ A) boosting greatly

_____ B) going down suddenly and quickly

_____ C) produced in bulk

3. Plenty of experts think the "no" vote has the power to <u>wipe</u> what little confidence remains in the markets.

_____ A) remove

_____ B) negotiate

_____ C) generate

4. Instead, the Treasury's first document <u>incited</u> opposition because it gave the department extraordinary powers.

_____ A) roused deliberately

_____ B) professed deliberately

_____ C) restrained tremendously

5. This could damp much of the popular <u>outcry</u>.

_____ A) serious criticism

_____ B) warm applause

_____ C) support

▶ *For questions 6-10, read the following statements, mark Y (for YES) if the statement agrees with the information given in the passage; N (for NO) if the statement contradicts the information given in the passage; NG (for NOT GIVEN) if the information is not given in the passage.*

_____ 6. Bailout bust could lead policy makers, particularly Treasury Secretary Henry Paulson, to draw up a plan that more directly addresses the factors causing the financial system to fall apart.

_____ 7. The market, upon seeing its details, may already have come to that conclusion that the bill was a great help to the banking system.

_____ 8. If a better-thought-out plan emerges in the coming days, stocks may stop shrinking.

_____ 9. The plan needed to be adapted to such an extent that the Congress would accept.

_____ 10. Though the approach carries large risks, half of the Congress members are firmly for it.

 **Section B**

Passage One

China's Economy Races On Despite Storms

China's economy grew by 10.6 percent in the first quarter, compared with the first three months of 2007, despite widespread disruption from ice storms and power cuts to industry and transport in January and February.

The gross domestic product rise, which was above a market consensus (共识) of just above 10 percent, means that Beijing is likely to continue tightening monetary policy in the coming months, while its big trading partners loosen credit.

After the release of the figures, the People's Bank of China, the central bank, raised the proportion of deposits that large commercial banks must keep with it by 0.5 percentage points to 16 percent—the 16th such increase since mid-2006.

Growth in the first quarter was down slightly compared with the final three months of 2007, when it stood at 11.7 percent, mainly due to the slowing pace of export growth and the impact of severe weather.

The good news on growth was moderated by persistent high inflation, which came in at an annual rate of 8.3 percent in March, according to official figures also released on Wednesday. Inflation hit an 11-year high of 8.7 percent in February.

Food prices rose by 21 percent in the first quarter, accounting for 6.8 percentage points of the 8 percent rise in the consumer price index in that period, and putting the government's 2008 target of 4.8 percent almost certainly out of reach.

"The Chinese economy is continuing to maintain steady, fast and sound development," Li Xiaochao, of the National Bureau of Statistics, said on Wednesday.

But Mr. Li acknowledged difficulties in meeting the official inflation target, saying it was "akin to an expectation or guidance".

Stephen Green, of Standard Chartered Bank[①] in Shanghai, said he suspected there had been "some smoothing" of the figures for GDP "to forestall criticism of the monetary tightening policy from industry and local governments".

He said the figure for GDP increase should have been lower, taking into account the "major drag" on growth from weaker export growth, lower industrial production and the impact of high inflation.

"A sharply slower GDP number would have triggered a lot more criticism from interest groups opposed to tight money," he said.

In the first period, China also recorded its first year-on-year quarterly fall in its trade surplus for three years, confirming a trend set in late 2007 when export growth began to wane.

The trade surplus expanded eightfold between 2004 and 2007, but is now peaking, albeit (尽管) at a high level, because of weakening demand in big markets such as the U.S. and Europe, and rising costs in China.

An appreciating currency, more expensive labor and land, and tighter enforcement of environmental regulations are all adding to Chinese manufacturers' cost base.

Both Goldman Sachs[②] and JPMorgan revised their full-year growth forecasts upwards in the light of Wednesday's GDP figure.

Andy Rothman, of CLSA[③] in Shanghai, said the fall in net exports "will be balanced by the continued health of the primary economic drivers, domestic investment and consumption".

Beijing had expected inflation to begin falling by mid-year as problems with the supply of pork and other basic foodstuffs were overcome. But the emerging global food crisis is likely to add to inflationary pressures.

(541 words)

Note:

① Standard Chartered Bank（渣打银行）在维多利亚女王的特许下于 1853 年建立。该银行由两家英国海外银行合并而成，分别是：英属南非标准银行 (the Standard Bank of British South Africa) 和印度新金山中国汇理银行 (1911 年后译名改为：印度新金山中国渣打银行 The Chartered Bank of India, Australia and China)。

② Goldman Sachs（高盛公司）1869 年创立于纽约曼哈顿，集投资银行、证券交易和投资管理等业务为一体，是华尔街上历史最悠久、经验最丰富、实力最雄厚的投资银行之一。

③ 里昂证券（CLSA Asia-Pacific Markets 里昂证券有限公司）于 1986 年创办，总部设于香港。法国的里昂集团（Credit Lyonnais）2003 年与法国农业信贷集团合并后，里昂证券成为农业信贷集团在亚太区投资银行的分支，主要从事证券经纪、投资银行及私人投资业务。

Exercises

For questions 1-5, there are three definitions below each underlined word in the passage. One definition is closest to its meaning. One definition has the opposite or nearly opposite meaning. The remaining definition has a completely different meaning. Label the definitions C for closest, O for opposite, and D for different.

1. The good news on growth was <u>moderated</u> by persistent high inflation.

    _____ A) diminished

    _____ B) recommended

    _____ C) developed

2. Stephen Green, of Standard Chartered Bank in Shanghai, said he suspected there had been "some smoothing" of the figures for GDP "to <u>forestall</u> criticism of the monetary tightening policy from industry and local governments".

    _____ A) prevent in advance

    _____ B) hit back

    _____ C) help

3. But Mr. Li <u>acknowledged</u> difficulties in meeting the official inflation target.

    _____ A) denied

    _____ B) admitted

    _____ C) destroyed

4. It was "<u>akin</u> to an expectation or guidance".

    _____ A) indifferent

    _____ B) different

    _____ C) similar

5. An <u>appreciating</u> currency, more expensive labor and land, and tighter enforcement of environmental regulations are all adding to Chinese manufacturers' cost base.

    _____ A) appearing

    _____ B) increasing in value

    _____ C) decreasing

▶ *Answer questions 6-10, according to the passage.*

6. Under what circumstances did China's economy increase by 10.6 percent in the first quarter of the year 2008?

_____

7. What is the difference between Beijing and its big trading partners?

_____

8. How many times has the People's Bank of China raised the proportion of deposits since mid-2006?

_____

9. What was the inflation rate in February and March?

_____

10. What is the emerging global food crisis likely to exert on China's inflationary pressures?

_____

How to Save Money in Hard Times?

Several people on Twitter[①] were talking about not being able to save money because they didn't earn enough. It actually made me laugh because I earn less than $15,000 per year at my business. I have a mortgage that is over 50% of my take-home-pay every month. I would be willing to bet that the people complaining easily earn twice as much as I do.

Somehow, I have managed to save more money in the past few months than I did when I was earning $70,000 a year. So what changed? Well, I have a confession (坦白). For most of my life, I have thought that saving was...boring. Yup! I'm embarrassed to admit it but I wonder how many other people feel that way.

Over the last year, saving money became a priority for me. I realized that it was no longer an option; I had to have an emergency fund. It is even more of a priority because my income is so low. When you have less than $300 a month to spend on groceries, electric, phone, and fuel, even having a flat tire could be financially crippling (造成严重损失的).

These are the ways that I have found that I cannot save money on my current income.

1. I cannot have an automatic withdrawal from my account. My checking account is way (非常地) too fragile with the balance usually hovering under $100 to have anything withdrawn automatically.

2. I cannot put a regular amount into savings monthly. My income is too irregular to plan on putting any certain amount on any certain day. I find that I miss the date or the amount and it de-motivates me from saving anything.

3. I cannot put large amounts into my savings account at one time. While I would love to save money in $100 chunks, I just can't do it. If I wait to save until I have a large amount, the money will never get there.

4. I cannot use Smarty Pig[②]. This has been a popular plan lately but with the restriction of having to close the account if you withdraw before you reach your goal. I just can't justify the trouble it would take to set it up in the first place.

5. I cannot reduce my expenses any more than I already have with one exception. I smoke. I wish I didn't but I do and I can't seem to quit right now. It's something to work on for the future as it's an expense that I hate and really want to get rid of. I have reduced it to less than a pack a day and am working on reducing it even more.

6. I can't have a payroll deduction (薪资扣除，个人所得税的一项) as I don't get paychecks. This is one of the drawbacks of being self-employed.

7. I can't save money by reducing my grocery bill. I am spending less than $100 per month on groceries now and I really can't see myself spending any less than that.

8. I cannot save money by giving up movies, cable, eating out or other entertainment. I have not had the cable TV connected for the last year. I don't go to the movies or eat out. I find my entertainment the old-fashioned way. I spend time with my friends and family, and believe me,

they are very entertaining.

9. I cannot save money by reducing my heating or cooling expense. I have found that my tolerance for keeping my thermostat (温度调节器) set low is 60 degrees in the winter. Any lower than that and I just can't function. I can't reduce air conditioning as I don't have it in this house.

10. I can't save money by reducing my fuel expenses as I have already cut back as much as I can. I go so far as to only make one trip into town per week. Right now, that is my trip to Richmond for foster care training. If I need something in town, I get it then or I don't get it.

So there you have it. I have tried most of the tips and tricks that are advised for saving money. It just won't work for me. So how do I manage to save money?   (741 words)

Note:

① Twitter 是一个利用无线网络、有线网络和通信技术进行即时通讯的网站，是微博客的典型应用。它允许用户将自己的最新动态和想法以短信息的形式发送给手机和个性化网站群，而不仅仅是发送给个人。

② Smarty Pig 是一个免费为用户量身定制省钱计划的网站。

Exercises

For questions 1-5, complete the sentences with the information given in the passage.

1. Several people on Twitter were talking about not being able to save money because _____.

2. Over the last year, saving money became a _____ for me.

3. I have reduced smoking to less than _____ and am working on reducing it even more.

4. I spent time with my friends and family, and believe me, they are _____ _____.

5. I have tried most of the _____ that are advised for saving money. It just won't work for me.

▶ *For questions 6-10, read the following statements, mark Y (for YES) if the statement agrees with the information given in the passage; N (for NO) if the statement contradicts the information given in the passage; NG (for NOT GIVEN) if the information is not given in the passage.*

_____ 6. I have managed to save less money in the past few months than I did when I was earning $70,000 a year.

_____ 7. When you have less than $300 a month to spend on groceries, electric, phone, and fuel, even having a flat tire could be financially crippling.

_____ 8. I can save money by giving up movies, cable, eating out or other entertainment.

_____ 9. My tolerance for keeping my thermostat set low is 50 degrees in the winter.

_____ 10. I can save money by reducing my children's education expense.

Key

Unit One

Section A

Passage One

1. 4-6 months old; left abandoned in the woods
2. skittish; needed to get used to the family members and his new environment
3. A little love, trust and patience
4. an area to sit and they get exercise going up and down the ramp
5. The kitchen
6. have the rabbit take a piece of food from his hand
7. N   8. N   9. N   10. NG

Passage Two

1. C   2. D   3. B   4. B   5. D   6. A   7. B   8. D
9. CDO   10. OCD

Section B

Passage One

1. Y   2. N   3. N   4. N   5. NG   6. Y
7. OCD   8. CDO   9. ODC   10. ODC

Passage Two

1. companionship, acceptance, emotional support and unconditional love during the time they share with the owners
2. denial, true sadness or grief, and acceptance
3. skip or repeat a stage, or experience the stages in a different order
4. the child may expect the pet's return and feel betrayed after discovering the truth
5. a loss of purpose and an immense emptiness
6. try interacting with friends and family, calling a pet loss support hotline, even volunteering at a local humane society
7. DOC   8. DOC   9. OCD   10. CDO

Unit Two

Section A

Passage One

1. B   2. B   3. A   4. D   5. A   6. C

7. N 8. N 9. Y 10. NG

Passage Two

1. N 2. N 3. NG 4. Y 5. N 6. N

7. waterfront promenade 8. Pearl of the Orient

9. Victoria Harbor 10. No. 3

Section B

Passage One

1. A 2. A 3. C 4. A 5. N 6. N

7. N 8. Y 9. N 10. NG

Passage Two

1. self-driving 2. apprehensive 3. dissolved 4. paradise

5. skyscraper 6. D 7. C 8. B 9. A 10. B

Unit Three

Section A

Passage One

1. DCO 2. COD 3. ODC 4. OCD 5. COD 6. DCO

7. Mainstreet, U.S.A.; Adventureland; Fantasyland; Tomorrowland

8. Cinderella Castle

9. the young at heart and to those who believe that when you wish upon a star, your dreams come true.

10. numerous classic and unique attractions the numerous views of the future

Passage Two

1. D 2. A 3. A 4. C 5. B 6. C

7. ODC 8. ODC 9. DCO 10. DOC

Section B

Passage One

1. Y 2. N 3. N 4. NG 5. N 6. Y 7. Y

8. enchanted realms of fantasy and adventure, yesterday and tomorrow

9. attempting to incorporate Chinese culture, customs, and traditions

10. 1.6 million

Passage Two

1. Y 2. NG 3. Y 4. N 5. N 6. Y

7. DCO 8. ODC 9. OCD 10. DOC

Unit Four

Section A

Passage One

1. landed
2. amiable; approachable
3. demanding
4. expectations
5. like-minded
6. dejected
7. recalcitrant
8. advancements
9. adage
10. love

Passage Two

1. moved
2. worsen
3. 67-year-old
4. deteriorate
5. floor
6. pastime
7. N
8. N
9. NG
10. Y

Section B

Passage One

1. Peking Opera is very vivid and she likes the melody best and expected to wear the fancy facial make up
2. extinction
3. 200 music, dance, art, acrobatics ; a symbolic expression of Chinese culture
4. the exam scores
5. history and ethical principles
6. N   7. N   8. N   9. NG   10. N

Passage Two

1. Y   2. N   3. N   4. N   5. NG
6. an educational program that provides instruction in both the student's native language and the language of the host country
7. three; start taking all their classes in English only
8. the former does not have the same time limits as trnsitional programs
9. read, write, and speak English
10. many students feel overwhelmed during the first two years

Unit Five

Section A

Passage One

1. Y   2. N   3. Y   4. Y   5. N
6. NG   7. Y   8. DCO   9. COD   10. CDO

Passage Two

1. N   2. N   3. NG   4. N   5. Y

6. the roads was easily blocked by rocks falling from the mountain

7. excitable; prone to attack

8. wait for a damage assessment by geologists

9. aftershocks; blocked roads

10. Sichuan, Sichuan and neighboring Ganse Province, just 20, about 62

Section B

Passage One

1. N	2. Y	3. N	4. N	5. NG	6. Y

7. convection of the rocks

8. movement of the overlying plates; the brittle portions of overlying plates; storing tremendous energy within the plates

9. spreading; convergent; transform

10. plunge

Passage Two

1. D	2. D	3. B	4. C	5. A
6. C	7. C	8. A	9. B	10. B

Unit Six

Section A

Passage One

1. CDO	2. DCO	3. ODC	4. CDO	5. DCO	6. CDO
7. NG	8. Y	9. N	10. Y		

Passage Two

1. N	2. Y	3. N	4. N	5. Y	6. NG

7. in the basement of his office building and on a telephone poles outside private houses

8. whether wiretaps were a form of search or not

9. went underground figuratively as well as literally

10. was indeed a search and therefore should be protected under the Fourth Amendment

Section B

Passage One

1. N	2. Y	3. NG	4. Y	5. N	6. N
7. OCD	8. DOC	9. COD	10. OCD		

Passage Two

1. N	2. Y	3. NG	4. N	5. N	6. N	7. Y

8. Responsibility   9. cease to be free   10. never completely lost

Unit Seven

Section A
Passage One

1. N 2. NG 3. N 4. Y 5. Y 6. N
7. COD 8. OCD 9. DOC 10. DOC

Passage Two

1. B 2. A 3. D 4. D 5. A 6. D 7. A 8. C

Section B
Passage One

1. 12% 2. the newly launched version of Internet Explorer / IE
3. a search box 4. 27 5. the option 6. Internet Explorer / IE
7. that browser/IE 8. a third

Passage two

1. N 2. Y 3. N 4. N 5. N 6. N
7. the emergency exit door 8. a piece of wire and a washcloth
9. *No Tech Hacking* 10. simple tricks

Unit Eight

Section A
Passage One

1. N 2. Y 3. N 4. N 5. Y 6. NG
7. DCO 8. ODC 9. CDO 10. DOC

Passage Two

1. CDO 2. OCD 3. CDO 4. CDO 5. CDO
6. Y 7. N 8. Y 9. Y 10. NG

Section B
Passage One

1. CDO 2. CDO 3. OCD 4. DOC 5. DCO

6. Under the circumstances of widespread disruption from ice storms and power cut to industry and transport in January and February.

7. Beijing is likely to continue tightening monetary policy in the coming months, while its big trading partners loosen credit.

8. 16.

9. 8.7 percent and 8.3 percent respectively.

10. The emerging global food crisis is likely to add to inflationary pressures.

Passage Two

1. they didn't earn enough   2. priority   3. a pack a day
4. very entertaining   5. tips and tricks
6. N   7. Y   8. N   9. N   10. NG